MJ FORSH

The Beast of the Kingswood

Copyright © 2025 by MJ Forsh

All rights reserved. No part of this publication may be reproduced, stored or transmitted in any form or by any means, electronic, mechanical, photocopying, recording, scanning, or otherwise without written permission from the publisher. It is illegal to copy this book, post it to a website, or distribute it by any other means without permission.

This novel is entirely a work of fiction. The names, characters and incidents portrayed in it are the work of the author's imagination. Any resemblance to actual persons, living or dead, events or localities is entirely coincidental.

First edition

ISBN: 979-8-9926673-0-1

Cover art by Jessica Cvilo

This book was professionally typeset on Reedsy.
Find out more at reedsy.com

For Steph–

Because being my sounding board for two decades, it's the least I could do

A Note from the Author

The Beast of the Kingswood is, much like myself, an unapologetically queer fantasy. This means it includes, but is not limited to:

- Trans Rights (and Trans Wrongs)
- Sex Work is Real Work
- **OPEN DOOR BEDROOM SCENES** between two men
- So much yearning
- Fantasy Typical Xenophobia
- Fantasy Typical Blood/Violence

To my fellow Aces: you're seen loved and valued. So, if you want to skip the Spice:

Skip to Chapter 9 after the scene break in Chapter 8

Skip to Chapter 12 after the scene break in Chapter 11

-MJ Forsh

1

Chapter 1

"There's my favorite freelance wild man. Aren't I the luckiest girl in the world? You're just the face I was hoping to see today!"

The chipper greeting almost had Alnyx turn and walk right back out the door he had barely made his way all the way through. The way his nearly empty coin purse hit his thigh convinced him otherwise.

"Yes, hello to you too Fish. Do you want a little snack?"

His traitor of a companion practically pushed his legs out from under him to get inside when their name and "snack" were said close enough together. The white and gray hound sat in front of the high counter, looking over its shoulder to Alnyx. He had no choice but to go in now.

"You have something for me then?" He grunted, the heavy door swinging closed behind him. "Potential for an unpleasant storm scared my last escort group off."

"Everyone loves the Divines until late autumn." The mortal girl behind the desk giggled when the hound stood on its hind legs and put its front paws on the counter, sniffing about for the promised treat. She took a piece of meat from the sandwich she had been eating out from between the bread and handed it over. "Have a fresh one, right off the Guild Master's pen. Good one too. Tracking work."

As troublesome as working within the Tasker guild could be, it meant there was always work to be done. The re-organization of what was formerly several Mercenary clans into a proper business model meant an end to meeting in dark allies and price gouging. The cut the guild took for "ensuring future contracts, burials, and general upkeep" might have been more than Alnyx would have liked, but it made sure all the work he *did* take was legitimate.

"What sort of tracking are we talking, Marigold?" The fact he remembered her name always kept him on the girl's good side. Which kept him top of mind for high-paying jobs when he rolled in.

"Came in from the Hunstmaster up in the Kingswood. Royal crest and everything. Apparently they've got a nasty beast of some kind on their hands that's scaring away all their game. Took out at least one of their men too."

Exactly up his alley. Alnyx held his hand out for the paperwork to sign and claim as she lifted it from the top of a pile. The way she paused and left her fingers on it when she set it on the desk had him arching an eyebrow.

"There is….One little thing. A Teeny, tiny, insignificant little change that came down from the top a about a fortnight ago. I tried to send a notice to you, but you're a hard man to track down you know…."

"A change?" Alnyx wrinkled his nose. "More fees? Whatever. Give me the new amount to sign off on."

"Not fees, for once." She laughed. "The Guild Master and council aren't allowing for solo contract work. After the incident with the Queen of Iris, all Taskers are on the Buddy System until further notice. Especially if they are, and I'm quoting here, without family and of an attractive face."

"Incident" was one way to put it. The Queen of Iris had hired a Tasker to serve as a private, personal guard when she took a trip to a temple on the far edge of her empire. Nine months later, a blond child was born to the raven-haired King and Queen.

"You're joking."

"Wish I was. Concessions had to be made to keep the office over there. Lots of work comes out of the region. All jobs are on a two Tasker minimum until a re-negotiation period. Exceptions are possible for extreme circumstances or a confirmed need of subtlety, with sign-off at time of acceptance from at least two thirds of the Council." She said the last part as if she had been made to memorize it off of a missive.

"And I'm assuming they haven't upped costs to a two plus to compensate."

He didn't ask it as a question, and she didn't answer it as one. They both knew.

"I don't suppose Fish can act as my second?"

"Not unless he'd stop you from impregnating a member of a monarchy."

Alnyx glanced down, as if he was going to ask the beast. He was smacking his maw, having eaten the bit of meat it had been given. The snort and way he flopped on the ground to lick its paws clean was answer enough. Bastard.

"Very well. You have a Resident of a Contractor in town you have in mind, I presume? Expedited for a crown and all, since I might not have been coming in."

"Gosh you're bright. And handsome. How issit there isn't a Missus wild elf yet?"

"Mister." Alnyx deadpanned with a shrug.

"Ugh! All the good ones are either married or wanna screw one another." She finally took her fingers off of the contract so he could sign it. "You know what, I DO have the perfect person. He's staying at the Snakehead Inn right now, and is on loan to us from the Scholars. Goes by Absinthe. The barkeep'll know him for sure."

"Absinthe." Alnyx repeated to himself, his signature on the acceptance line more a scribble than proper letters. "Thank you, Marigold."

"Sure thing. You come back safe now. Need my favorite eye candy." She winked and giggled again when Fish stood with a single bark. "And I'll make sure to have a proper treat for Fishy Fish next time too."

* * *

The Snakehead wasn't one of Alnyx's usual haunts when he stayed at the Port. It was closer to the old part of the settlement, where there was money and politicians instead of normal, working folks. The Inn itself was the sort where your coin got you a room all to yourself instead of a bed-share in a bunk room. It wasn't the sort of place he was normally granted entry into. Definitely not with Fish next to him.

He and the hound looked at one another as they stood in front of the door. It was emblazoned with a mosaic of some sort of cobra, its hood fanned out as it looked ready to strike. If you couldn't read the sign over it, it made it obvious where you were.

"Go. We'll meet you." Alnyx rolled his eyes when he got a growl and bark in return. "Don't give me that. You don't want to go inside. You aren't missing anything."

The head tilt said the wolf wasn't sure they agreed. Neither of them broke eye contact for a long moment, mossy brown meeting the ever-ethereal and glowing blue of the beast. Finally Fish huffed a snort of air from his nose and turned his head.

"It will be quick. South gate."

A lick to fingers that were exposed from gloves that were cut off from the top knuckle upward. A scratch behind furry ears. The wolf walked down the street like it was meant to be there, and the others around gave it a wide berth. Alnyx watched until Fish turned a corner and disappeared from view.

Alnyx paused to look at his reflection in the window beside the door before going inside. His chestnut hair was long overdo for a trim, but he had recently shaved the sides back down to the skin. The rest was tied up and away from his face, and was as clean as a few days on the road allowed. The swirls of black and gray ink that started on the sides of his head trailed down his throat and further beyond what the leather armor covered. The black of the skins matched the bands of ink around the tips of his ears, and his fingers as he reached up to adjust the claw that was pierced through one of the lobes. No matter how well he could clean it, the tattoos were what often got him the scoff from desk workers at places like this. Perhaps he should have stopped to clean his face properly, the kohl that normally lined his eyes *was* a smudgy mess at the moment.

Not that any of that stopped him from just walking in to places before, and it wasn't going to this time. He was just...Not in the mood for an argument about being "civilized" this morning.

"Just a quick in and out." He said to himself, shaking his head and using the side of a finger to wipe away some of the errant kohl.

He pulled the door open and the world did not stop spinning. The mortal behind the counter scowled and gave him a long look up and down, clearly having been watching since he stopped at the window. The distaste was evident without either of them needing to say a word. It usually was with mortals like this one, who kept their fingernails as clean as the counter top that they drummed them on.

"Just looking for someone." He held up his hands to show they were empty, even if the scabbards at his sides were very much not. "Bar?"

"Don't cause trouble, Blade-Ear. I won't hesitate to toss you back out where you belong." They lifted one hand and pointed to an open doorway over to the right.

The insult had stopped phasing Alnyx a decade ago. At best, it was an observation that anyone with sight could make, at worst a bastardized translation of words in his native tongue. He'd heard the mortals call other Bloodlines worse things. So, he rolled his shoulders back and held his chin up higher as he went through the doorway that was pointed to.

It was busier than he would have thought it might be, considering the early hour. People with money didn't have to labor while there was sun to do work by, he supposed. All the fine fabrics and perfume in the room said the people at the tables here certainly fell into the "more money than sense" category. He wrinkled his nose as the cloud of scents was particularly potent at the table he had to walk by, several men all with at least one woman on their laps and arms around their necks. Alnyx recognized one of the women from his usual bar. Good for her. Hope she was charging him a premium.

She gave him a wink when they made eye contact. It was easily missed by the man whose lap she occupied, who was more than transfixed by how low the cut of her bodice was. Alnyx nodded to the man behind the bar as he approached, sitting on one of the high stools furthest from the crowded center of the room.

"Get you something Sir?" He asked and walked to stand across from him. "Ale, wine, spirits?"

"Information. Looking for someone, and Marigold said you could point me to him."

"Well then. A Friend of Mari's is a friend of mine." The man took the towel off of his shoulder, wiping the bar-top down before speaking again with a lowered voice. "Who is it you're looking for?"

"Contractor. Goes by Absinthe." He wished he had gotten any sort of description to go off of. "She seemed quite certain that the name would be enough."

"Ah, that one." The man chuckled. "You're a few bells too early for them to be out and about. Quite the night owl."

Of course he was. Mages always making things difficult. He was doubting more and more that this Spirit-named scholar was really the "perfect person" for a fight with a mystery beast. Clearly, Marigold was either playing some sort of joke on him or this was in response to him rebuffing her advance. Alnyx barely managed not to groan.

"A few bells you said?"

"Two at the very least." The barman sounded apologetic. "You're welcome to wait here for 'em if you want. First one's on me. Friend of Marigold and all."

When the tankard of ale was slid to him from across the bar, Alnyx caught sight of a tattoo on the inside of the man's wrist. Black and green, the bud of a rose faded with time and sun. A mark shared by one of the original mercenary clans, uncommon outside of prison cells and cemeteries nowadays. A nod in appreciation and acknowledgment, returned in kind before the man went to go refill drinks for one of the tables.

At least two bells. Fish wasn't going to be pleased, at all. Alnyx made a mental note to step by one of the butcher shops to get a few good bones and maybe a bit of liver as an apology.

2

Chapter 2

It was closer to three bells than two before the barman walked over to Alnyx. He had been staring into his second mostly empty tankard for the better part of the last one. At some point, the rowdiest of the tables had cleared out and there was some semblance of silence again. He could hardly hear himself think before they left.

"Absinthe's coming in now." the barman said. "I'll flag them over for you and make introductions."

Alnyx knocked back the last slosh of lukewarm ale and nodded a thank you. He didn't turn to look right away, gathering his will to be cordial before they approached. There was the unmistakable tapping of heeled boots across the wooden floor as the figure came closer.

"Cinna, my good man." The voice was warm, an accent he could only place as vaguely western in origin. "Brightmarrow be blessed if you've already got my tea ready."

"You're a creature of habit, Absinthe." the barman chucked, already pouring steaming tea into a delicate bone china cup. A splash of a dark liquor went in with it, the scent of herbs quickly covered by the spirit. "You've a caller this afternoon. Alnyx, this is Absinthe."

Alnyx finally turned his head, to see only gray-violet flesh. The cut of the cream colored shirt was open practically to the navel. Tall, lean, toned in the slim-muscled way many mages were. Their powers ate away at any extra energy and resource their body could provide, often in the form of extra fat. He could feel the flush hit his cheeks, as if he was seeing something he wasn't meant to. Veins and scars trailed up the flesh, though it was easy for him to be able to tell the difference between the two: the individual's veins were an acidic green against the strangely colored skin. Alnyx would bet the coin left in his purse, they would glow when magic was used.

When he finally looked up to see the face, he felt himself swallow and hoped it hadn't made a sound. A sharp jaw and a squared chin. The green didn't end with the veins, as their eyes were also green, corner to corner with no white of pupil. Like two pools of acid, the centers a slightly darker hue so you knew where they were looking. And that was directly at Alnyx. The piercing intensity of it almost made him miss the curved horns that came from their forehead. They bent backward and flared in opposite directions at the tips. The chitin of them was green at the base and faded to midnight black at their tips.

An elemental? A devil of Sanguine? A voidling? A blending of all three the elf had never seen before?

And beautiful. His traitorous mind provided. Alnyx shook his head, as if to forcibly be rid of the thought.

"A gentleman caller while the sun is still out? What sort of person do you take me for, Cinna?" They winked at the elf. "Another of whatever he's drinking, on my tab would you, Dear?"

Absinthe took a seat in the stool directly next to Alnyx. They crossed their impossibly long legs, turning so their back leaned against the bar as they settled. The elf watched them sip from the tea cup they had been handed before the new tankard was set down.

"How can I assist you, Mister Alnyx?" their black claws tapped a little beat against the porcelain.

"*You're* a contractor for the Taskers?" He hadn't meant for it to sound so....Incredulous. But this person didn't fit "scholar on loan" in the slightest.

"Is that what you're here for?" they sighed, a twinge of disappointment in it. "On occasion, yes. But if it's help you need, you'll need to put in a contract directly at the office." Absinthe cocked their head to the side. "But by the looks of you, you seem....Quite capable of handling problems all on your own."

"No." Alnyx grunted which got a chuckle that he wasn't prepared for in response. "I already have a contract." He couldn't manage more than one full thought at a time it seemed. So, he took a swig of ale before trying again.

"Marigold sent him over to find you." Cinna was apparently amused enough to stay close by to listen while cleaning glasses, and beat him to it. "Three bells ago, actually."

"Oh!" The verdant eyes widened and they set the tea cup down between themselves and Alnyx on the bar. "You should have sent someone to wake me!" They directed to the barman.

"You sent the last person who tried to the healers with burns. Not to mention they had to replace the door and door frame to your room." Cinna shook his head. "You'll pardon me if I didn't want a repeat."

"He's exaggerating." Absinthe turned their attention back to Alnyx. "A contract. And you need a second because the horny bastard in Iris tarnished the guild's reputation."

"Right." Alnyx bent down to pull the contract from his bag he had taken from his back at some point while waiting. "Royal seal, makes sharing the coin more tolerable." He offered it up to Absinthe to look at.

"High paying contract and Marigold trusted you to just walk out without a guarantee I'd come along? Color me impressed, Mister Alnyx."

"Just Alnyx."

Another little chuckle, and Absinthe took the paper in one hand and their teacup back up in the other. Just as Marigold had said: some sort of unknown beast was scaring and killing game in the Kingswood belonging to the royals of Pugila a short trip from the Port. Head of the beast or some tangible proof of its demise mandatory for payment, to be brought to the Huntsmaster in the camp at the edge of the wood.

"And you're sure Marigold meant for you to look for me?" They wrinkled their nose and handed the paper back. "Not that I don't trust you. I'm sure it comes as no surprise that monster hunting is not typically the sort of job I take on."

"Specifically said you. Probably knows something we don't." Alnyx bent and returned the contract to his bag.

"Ah now that sounds like her." They took a last sip of their spirit-laced tea and sighed in a way that had Alnyx swallowing again. "All right. You've peaked my interest, Just Alnyx. Let me settle up at the desk and gather my things. Be back in a tick."

Alnyx didn't mean to stare when Absinthe walked away, truly. The long black coat, embroidered with flowers and flames with fine, silver, thread simply distracted him when it brushed against him with the way the horned individual flourished as they rose and left. The long drink he took afterwards was simply a coincidence of momentary dry mouth.

Just coincidence. He repeated in his mind when he heard Cinna laugh behind the bar again. Alnyx remained just long enough to finish his drink before grabbing his bag and going back out to the entrance lobby.

* * *

"So sorry about that. Ready to head out?"

Alnyx had been waiting in the lobby for Absinthe to return once they went up to get their belongings and coin to settle paying for the room. A single bag across their back, well kept and made of nicely conditioned leather. Just a glance at the clothing they wore, it seemed...Too small for their belongings.

The clothes were noticeably different than what they had been wearing before they went up the stairs. The long coat was gone, and the low cut tunic had been exchanged as well. Clothes more practical for travel, a rough-spun and made to keep warm and dry, and a coat that came only to the backs of their knees instead of their ankles. Though the boots still had more of a heel than Alnyx ever would have considered outside a ball.

"Here you are my good man." Absinthe held an envelope out to the human behind the counter Alnyx had been having a glaring contest with while he waited. "The Scholar liaison will be here to collect the rest of my belongings before the dinner bell."

That made more sense. The mortal looked over the note inside the envelope and nodded once.

"Very good, sir." it didn't go unnoticed how the man was very deliberate in only touching exactly what was needed after Absinthe handled it.

Alnyx was certain as soon as they were out the door, he was going to be taking soap and water to everything they touched. He bit his tongue, holding the door open for Absinthe who grinned and whispered a soft "thank you, Dear" before leaving.

"I have a stop to make before we go. Through the market." Alnyx said, walking beside Absinthe who arched an eyebrow.

"You need to stop for supplies? I'm sure between the two of us we can manage the trip."

"I have a companion. He is waiting for us outside the gates. I had told them that it wouldn't take very long..."

"Oh." Absinthe's blush was not rosy, which made sense. A tinge of green graced the high cheek bones. "Really. Cinna should have sent someone for me. But if you have a companion, why did you need to come and ask me to join you? Not that I'll argue over good coin."

"They are a hound."

"A hound. And what, you have them just tethered to a tree outside the walls?" They snorted a laugh. "I don't think I would have pegged you for the pet type."

"I didn't say he was a pet. They are my Watcher." Alnyx wasn't surprised at the blink he got in response from the Mage. "What is it that the mages call them...Familiars. He is like the familiars that the scholars of my Kin carry. I am of the woods and the mountains, not the ivory towers and floating cities. My people do not keep ferrets or mice."

"Not from the floating cities. I suppose that explains the fetching tattoos of yours." Absinthe took their time looking Alnyx up and down, as if they hadn't considered anything but the elves they were used to. "So what are you called then? I assume Weave-Eyed or ley-blood don't really apply."

"They do not, no. Ancestry is the only thing we share anymore." Alnyx shook his head. "We are known as Wild Elves or Grove Wardens by those who ask the difference. Rawanali."

"A lovely word." Absinthe couldn't quite accent it properly, but they made an effort. He had heard far worse. "Go on. Ask. I can tell you want to. Everyone does."

As they entered the busy marketplace square, both instinctively had a hand on their coin purses. The scholar had self preservation. Good. Alnyx approached the butcher and handed over coins for a few decent sized bones, and a vertebrae of a beast with a good bit of marrow in it. The grisly treat would get him Fish's forgiveness. Business taken care of, he took the lead towards the South Gate.

"You are a voidling. What is it called here...Star-crossed?"

"A better first guess than I usually hear!" Absinthe beamed but shook their head. "Usually I get satyr. Or that my mother must have fucked some sort of Hells-Cursed Goat. Though really those two are basically the same thing."

Alnyx could not stop the chuckle as they went on. More than he was usually give in response.

"My mother was a Wylder. If you're from the woods, I'm sure you've met them before. Nomadic human cults. Hers were green mages, worshiping the Divines that gave them their magic, so she'd say."

"I have met many Wylders." Alnyx confirmed. " You said half. Your... Father then."

"Mmhm, never met the man. I assume he's where these came from." they gestured to their horns. "Otherwise my mother did a flawless job hiding hers."

That made some sense. The Wylders he knew were lacking...Charm, and the sensibilities Absinthe seemed to carry. He found it hard to imagine this person with their long coat and tea with their spirits in a caravan.

"I left as soon as I could find traders that would take me with them. Never much got in to ancestor worship and hoping to be reborn as like...A mountain lion or a tree. No offense meant, but it was never really for me."

Alnyx shook his head instead of giving an answer. It wasn't worth giving an explanation of his clan's traditions to someone he was not going to see again after this fortnight. He looked over, to see Absinthe's head tilted to the side, similar to when Fish saw or smelled something interesting.

"Not a man of many words, are you, Alnyx? I suppose if you usually travel with a hound, it can't be helped." They sighed. "Not to worry. I'm often told I can speak enough for three."

This sort of teasing normally annoyed Alnyx. He was too quiet. Too stoic. He had heard it all from people he escorted along the trails. But, Absinthe really did just go on like the two of them were having a conversation that went both ways. Strange. But not wholly unpleasant.

"Right then." Absinthe stopped mid-story as they got outside the gate, glancing around. "Let's see this not-a-pet then."

Of course, Fish wasn't just sitting somewhere out in the open. Too often, people got curious and nosy when they were without Alnyx. And too often, it was curiosity that led to stupidity or violence. Alnyx put two fingers into his mouth and let out a shrill whistle in four sharp bursts. After a moment, the bush to the left of them up the path rustled and the blue-eyes beast padded out as if it had been there the whole time.

"A hound." Absinthe's laugh caught Alnyx off guard. "That is no hound. That is an Arctic Lycine. Fully grown and very, very far from home might I add."

"Not many know what he is, so hound is easiest." Alnyx shrugged to hide that he was a little impressed that Absinthe knew at a glance. He offered up the vertebrae to Fish as a silent apology. "It will not be a problem?"

"A problem...No, no." the little chuckle again. "What...I mean, does it have a name? Fae beasts are known for stealing them."

"Fish."

"A...Canine named Fish?" Alnyx gave a single nod in response to the question. "What a strange elf you are, Just Alnyx."

Alnyx felt heat creep up his neck an d ears. Especially when Fish, treat in mouth, padded closer to Absinthe to inspect them. A sniff of their hand, he found them acceptable enough it seemed

"We need to get moving." Alnyx said before the embarrassment could settle in. "We need to find a suitable camp before it gets too late. Won't be getting to the Kingswood today."

"Of course. Lead the way."

* * *

Alnyx was pleasantly surprised with how easily Absinthe was able to keep up pace with him. When it got warmer midday, they had removed the long coat and folded it into the bag, without pausing to rearrange anything inside it. It didn't make the bag bulge even a little, and the elf couldn't help but arch an eyebrow.

"Bigger than it looks." Absinthe winked as they pulled the straps back over their shoulders. " Magic has to have some perks after all."

Alnyx shook his head a little, but silenced again as they continued along. They didn't stop until they came across the stream that would eventually cut through the woods they were on their way towards. The lycine snapped a fish up from the water and swallowed it in practically a single bite, looking quite pleased with themselves as they did so.

"I suppose it wouldn't be cannibalism if it's just your name, huh?" Absinthe pondered while the beast shook water from its fur.

The exhale of air from Alnyx's nose was as close as he normally allowed himself to a laugh, the mage was learning quickly. Sure, the elf wasn't exactly a charmer, but he didn't have to be for the line of business he was in. Perhaps, though, he wasn't half as dour as the frown lines and silence made it seem.

They veered up along the stream from the trade road they had been following. Absinthe continued the aimless chatter they had started back in the city. Long periods of silence left them feeling unsettled, they explained. Too many years in temple services or libraries, where it was strictly enforced. If Alnyx was bothered by it, he at least kept it to himself.

By the time the sky began to darken and the temperature dropped, they managed to find a suitable site to settle inset camp for the night. Char marks on the ground and flattened earth said they weren't the first to think as much. They removed their packs to set out bedrolls for the evening, Fish already circling to settle in a spot near where the fire would eventually be.

"I can get a fire going." Absinthe offered, removing their boots and stretching their legs out. "Don't suppose I could talk you in to seeing if there's anything worth hunting out there? Trail rations are always dreadful."

The grunt said it was fine by him. He hadn't taken off the harness that made up the scabbards where his two short-swords were housed, so he didn't have to worry about getting it back on.

"Not on crown lands yet, shouldn't be a problem. Did you want to get wood first then?"

"Wood? Oh I don't need all that." Absinthe grinned and shook their head. "Just a little bit of space and a pinch of phosphorescence."

Alnyx arched an eyebrow as Absinthe dug into the bag at their side, finally withdrawing a maroon colored pouch. They withdrew a palm-sized clear crystal, dusted with a yellow powder that the pouch was likely full of. Absinthe set it on the ground, at the center of the charred earth, rubbing the powder from their fingers into the palm of their left hand.

Standing up straight again, they held their hand out with the dusty palm towards the ground. Wherever there was usually green on the mage's body flashed a bright white, and the air around them grew thick and warm for a moment. As both heat and white faded, there was a spark from the crystal like striking flint to tinder. There was no physical flame but the glow from the crystal produced heat and light like one would have. Alnyx wiggled their fingers as a "ta-dah" before wiping their hands on their pants.

"Little trick I picked up when I was up north a few years ago. Hard to find dry wood there, since it's mostly ice and stone. I don't do cold well."

"Hmm." Alnyx bent down, holding his hand over where the light was brightest. It was hot enough, but didn't burn his skin like flame would have. "You can cook over it?"

"Takes a little longer. Small price to pay to avoid the smoke though. I take it you don't travel with magic users normally?"

"Don't travel with anyone usually." The growl from Fish seemed to indicate that the lycine took offense to not being considered a someone. "I'll see what game there is."

"Fantastic. I'll make sure our bags stay safe. I'm excellent at minding camp."

Alnyx shook his head, and Absinthe was certain they saw a smile. The elf disappeared into the shadows at the edge of the campsite quickly, and Fish made absolutely no effort to follow along.

"Going to keep me company are you?" Absinthe flopped back onto their bed roll, legs stretched out before them and leaning back on their elbows. "Can't blame you. I'm well exhausted from all this running around. Wasn't exactly planning on a wilderness hike when I woke up."

It was hard to tell if Fish learned the snort from Alnyx, or the other way around. It was absolutely darling all the same. Lycines were fearsome creatures, as far as the bestiaries Absinthe had read were concerned. They were the product of exposure to ley lines and concentrated mana slowly mutating native species. Invasive in some areas, known to hunt livestock and people if there were no other options. But the big yawn and shake of the head warmed Absinthe's heart. Not quite a tender beast, but Absinthe was not concerned it was going to attack them in their sleep. An anomaly. Not unlike the elf that was his not-master.

"You two are odd things, aren't you?" Fish peaked open a blue, glowing eye. "Oh not to worry, I am too. Takes one to know one, doesn't it?"

They were certain that the lycine understood. If the texts in the scholar library were correct, they were highly intelligent creatures. Perhaps their physicality and body structure didn't allow them to speak as two-legged beasts could, but it was widely accepted that they could decipher it. Some of them were known to be able to solve puzzles and mazes of varying difficulties.

The way Fish turned his head to start chewing on the inside of his leg made Absinthe reconsider.

The evening passed in quiet company once Alnyx returned. Two decently sized hares, which once properly dressed Absinthe took over cooking. The elf took their time oiling the blades and leathers he wore before using a brush to get tangles and loose hair out of Fish's fur. Absinthe settled with a text of some kind balanced on their knees, scooting closer to the magicked light to make reading it easier.

They whispered the words out loud to themselves as they read, audible only as a string of sound from where Alnyx sat on the other side of the glow. The elf could feel the corners of his lips curl into a smile.

He was not besotted with this odd creature. He was not. Fish snorted, as if he heard Alnyx's thought.

"Shut up." he grumbled at the beast, smacking its haunch with no real force or malice.

"Pardon?"

"Not you." Alnyx winced, knowing he responded far too quickly. "Him. You...You're fine."

"Flattery will get you everywhere."

Not. Besotted.

3

Chapter 3

Moving at the decent clip they were, they managed to get to the camp of the Royal Huntsmen of Pugila before sundown the next day. There was a larger, permanent cabin, whose chimney smoke made it easy to find the site. It was clearly where the King or his guests usually stayed, but would be empty except for staff right now. Potential Hell Beasts often kept nobility away.

"Halt, travelers." The guard at the entrance to the camp held one hand out to stop them, the other resting on the hilt of their sword. "These are the King of Pugila's woods. State your business."

The human's suspicious gaze wasn't sure where it wanted to settle. Horns, pointed ears, and a beast with glowing eyes. The three of them were walking alarm bells for those not used to anything outside of boiler plate humanity. Alnyx's lip curled into a snarl, and he readied himself to move on the defensive.

"Yes, of course my good man." Absinthe spoke before he could get them in trouble. "We've been sent by the Tasker Guild over in Port Morgranto. Seems your captain organized a contract to give you all a hand with a monster."

"And you have this contract." The placed, disgusted, emphasis even had Absinthe's clearly practiced smiled falter for a moment.

"Naturally. Alnyx?"

Since the mark on the contract was his, he had kept it in his bags after they left the city. Ages ago, when Alnyx first started taking these sorts of jobs, he'd invested in an envelope. The treated water-proof parchment with an embossed sigil of the guild made it look more professional then the job normally was. And it was instrumental in shutting down bigots like this one. He held the envelope out once he withdrew it.

"All there." he grunted, managing to swallow the growl when the guard took it none too gently. Not quite rough enough to be a "snatch" but it wasn't far off.

Alnyx looked to Absinthe and couldn't help rolling his eyes. Absinthe's head shake and shrug in response was a "what can you do?" from someone just as used to this sort of treatment. Humans had a nasty little superiority complex. Give them a weapon and a modicum of power in a situation? Don't even get the elf started.

"Right gentlemen. All seems to be in order." He handed the envelope back to Alnyx, but the hand still remained on his sword. "The Huntsmaster is in his tent. Red one at the center of the camp. You keep that out and show it to anyone that asks. And don't cause trouble."

Did all the stupid ones just assume that Alnyx liked having to defend himself? That non-humans got off on riling up a crowd? The snarl he had hoped he had hidden away clearly showed through with how quickly the man pulled his hand back.

"Thank you, good hunter." Absinthe broke the tension with a nod, tapping Alnyx's arm before leading them into the camp. "You have an absolutely terrible poker face. I can only hope you never make bets." They laughed when the three of them were out of earshot.

"I have a low tolerance for stupidity. Especially from someone who does not know me or is not paying me."

"So I can see. You catch more flies with honey."

"I would rather crush the flies."

"So ferocious." they chuckled. "I'd rather avoid a fight. But I suppose between the two of us, you are the one with the swords and I'm not."

Alnyx gave no reply, as he noticed the hunters around them pausing in the work they were supposed to be doing to glance their way. A few outright staring. By the time they reached the red tent that had been mentioned, a man with a heavy cloak and an air of importance was in front of it. The rifle slung across their back marked them as the Huntsmaster.

"Taskers aye? Quicker than I thought. Good. Hunstmaster Bennett." He properly introduced himself.

"Absinthe. This is Alnyx." they gestured between the two of them and Fish barked once. "I was getting to you. The furry one is Fish."

"Come in." Bennett seemed unbothered by the creature, a definite point in the good column. "I'll catch you up on what we know so far." He walked back into the tent through the open flap, not looking behind to see if they followed.

It wasn't much, but the thick fabric muffled the sounds outside of it and made it so they could speak more freely. There were a few proper pieces of furniture inside, denoting it as a more permanent fixture of the camp than the smaller tents. An armor-stand on one side of the space currently housed a set of well-maintained plate armor, and there was a desk scattered with maps and notes they couldn't read from the entrance. The full sized, fur-laden bed was the greatest luxury.

"We first spotted the beast after the last dark moon. Near one of the caves at the center of the King's portion of the woods." Bennett said as he walked to the desk, brushing some of the papers away from the large map. "One of our forward scouts got just close enough to see it wasn't natural. Not something they'd ever seen."

"If it is some ley-based beast, that wouldn't be a surprise." Absinthe followed, arms crossed as they looked down at the desktop. "The empty sky of the Dark Moon is said to allow certain ones greater movement."

"We've tracked its movement for the last two fortnights. None of the scouts want to get any closer than they have to."

"Guild mentioned one of yours got mauled." Alnyx joined them, using a finger to trace the colored pins that marked sightings.

"One of the trainees and their instructor. Instructor got the worst of it. Didn't make it. I told them to wait, but they didn't listen. Headstrong." Bennett sighed. "Body was half eaten by the time we could get to it. Kid climbed up into a tree and it didn't bother him up there.

"Half eaten?" Absinthe wrinkled their nose. "So, not a herbivore then. Sound familiar to you, Alnyx?"

"What does it look like? Horns, wings?" when the Huntsmaster shook his head at both, Alnyx arched an eyebrow. "Claws? Monstrous jaws?"

"That's the problem we've run in to. Every scout I send out comes back with a different description. Some of them have said a bear, some a boar. The trainee said an elk, and the fact the instructor looked like she had been gored, we had to agree."

"A shapeshifter then. Narrows it down more than you might think." Absinthe ran the tip of their claw along the marks on the map, leaning forward over them. "We find its den, we can get it in its natural state. They're weaker then."

Alnyx couldn't argue with the logic. But looking at the potential sighting locations, it was a lot of ground to cover with just two of them. It didn't seem likely they would get volunteers to come along. Potentially getting killed by a mystery ley-beast was outside the paid responsibility of a hunter.

"Any reports you can provide would be helpful." Alnyx looked to Bennett. "Might be able to make some sense of things. And a map like this with all the sightings if you can spare it, so we can figure out best where to go first."

"I'll have them to you by the evening meal. Need to make sure nothing in there you shouldn't see." strangers to their King after all. "The trainee is still at the medical tent. Tell the healer I sent you to talk to him."

A dismissal without being specifically told to go. Alnyx nudged Absinthe when the scholar didn't move right away. The wordless acknowledgment should have been unsettling. But it was instead comfortable when they both stepped back at the same time. They walked out where Absinthe was a half step behind him, and a half step in front of Fish. Slotting into the spot like they were made for it.

Alnyx swallowed the bubble of warmth before he could risk it causing him to say something foolish. The walk across the campsite to the medical tent was a quick one, with people giving them a wide berth. Once they arrived, the young hunter-to-be eyed them warily, mostly Fish. Understandably really, given the last unfamiliar beast they came across killed a man in front of them.

Once the healer explained they were here to help, the young man seemed much more willing to tell them what he knew. The beast had taken the shape of a large elk, which hadn't been so out of the ordinary for the Kingswood. But, the fact it was black as soot, with jagged antlers and a "foul air" had tipped them off that something wasn't quite right.

It wasn't much to go on, but the young hunter confirmed that the beast had been alone, and didn't seem to be protecting any sort of mate or cubs or any such thing. Knowing there was just one of them was at least some sort of relief.

Absinthe and Alnyx decided it would be best for the two of them to part ways, to see what else they could gather from the scouts and hunters scattered across the camp. Perhaps a bias of his own upbringing and time among his Brothers and Sisters of the bow, Alnyx walked to where a small group of the hunters were shooting at targets and fetching arrows. A few arched eyebrows but when he picked up one of the strung bows, they couldn't help but take more interest.

He would always favor his blades, one of the many fights he had gotten in to with his cousins leading up to his departure from The Grove. That didn't mean he hadn't gone through the same training and education they had. He gave the string a tug back to feel the tension of it first before notching an arrow. Drawing back properly and taking a moment to aim, he fired and split the shaft already sticking out closest to the center on the middle ranged target.

"Here for the beast problem, yeah?" one of them leaned on their longbow in a way that Alnyx could hear his ancestors screaming over. "What do you need to know?"

* * *

When it came time for the evening meal, Alnyx walked to the bonfire with the archers. They hadn't given him anything new in terms of information, but the practice had felt good. The underused muscles from a lengthy marksmanship competition burned pleasantly. When he didn't see Absinthe in the gathered circle, he frowned.

"Your mage went off to study." Bennett was the one who handed him a battered looking bowl of some sort of thick stew. "Gave him the reports when I saw him with our trackers not that long ago. Tent with the blue and black flag's yours for the night."

"Thanks." Alnyx more grunted than spoke, taking a seat on one of the logs that were felled to be benches.

Once he had his fill, and made sure to pick a few choice pieces of the meat for Fish, he went to the person managing the stew, who happened to be the healer they had met at earlier. They were happy to hand over a helping for Absinthe since they hadn't made their way over. And even managed to scrounge up a decent bone for the lycine. Alnyx couldn't help but smile a little, watching as Fish gave his best attempt at a skip as he trotted ahead with the deer femur in his jaws to find the tent they had been allowed use of for the night.

Sure enough, he nearly tripped over Absinthe's knee-high boots inside the entrance of the canvas tent. The horned figure themselves was sitting, cross legged on one of the cots with paperwork scattered around on the rest of it. A lantern was lit on a post beside them, true fire and not one made with their crystal trick.

They didn't even look up. As if they hadn't heard Alnyx enter, or Fish jump up on the other cot and start at their bone. It took Alnyx holding the bowl directly in front of them, breaking the line of sight they had to the words, to get Absinthe to finally look up.

"Eat." He all but put it in their hands over the papers. "I don't need you being weak with hunger come morning, since we will be hiking."

The way those big, glowing eyes blinked said they were caught more off guard by the not quite command but more harsh than Alnyx had meant request. They slowly put the papers they held in a stack to the side and took the bowl from.

"A pet owner and the mothering type. Don't you continue to surprise?" Absinthe laughed when Alnyx's eyes narrowed. "Joking, joking."

The three settled into the same easy silence as they had at the camp site on the road: Fish with his bone, Absinthe with a single-minded focus on the stew until the bowl was empty, and Alnyx looking over his gear to ensure he would be prepared for a fight. He dug a needle and thread out of a side pouch of his bag to deal with a small hole in one of his gloves. Always mouthing the words, as if they couldn't stop their lips from moving for too long or they might forget to breathe, it was clear Absinthe barely touched their meal. Alnyx looked up from threading his needle, watching them as they went on. If they noticed the gaze, they didn't say anything about it.

"What do I call you?"

The elf's question got Absinthe's attention quicker than the stew had. The arched eyebrow and look of something between confusion and annoyance almost made Alnyx swear out loud. Inelegance was the cruelest curse the Ancestors could have touched his bloodline with.

"Earlier, the stupid guard said gentlemen and you said nothing. At the bar, Cinna never said he. Kept saying they. Marigold....You know her. So....What do I call you?"

The annoyance left Absinthe's eyes almost immediately. Reports set to the side and turning to face Alnyx, the elf couldn't help but notice the way the dim light from the lantern softened their features. All but the glow of their eyes.

"Have you been thinking about that this whole time?" The lack of an answer said more than words. "You sweet man."

This smile was different than the others Alnyx had seen them give. It was a crooked thing, showing teeth between full lips. They had jagged edges to them when you took the time to look at them. Like they were made to tear and rip flesh from bone. The low light caught every groove, but it wasn't menacing or ferocious when paired with the curl at the corners of the lips.

"I suppose it depends on the question you are trying to ask." Absinthe continued after they had a moment to think. "Do you mean to ask if I have a....Wand or a regent pouch?"

It took nearly as long of a moment of silence for Alnyx to piece the terribly lewd joke together. He looked quickly away, as if he had to stare each stitch of his mending down like an enemy for it to stick.

"Sorry, sorry. I couldn't help it. I come equipped with a wand in hand, not unlike your own sword I imagine. But, I don't hold myself only to that. A reagent pouch. A crystal. Sometimes, no tool at all."

"So you....Call yourself He then?" Alnyx looked back up again, lips pursed into a frown.

"It's a word that they" the gesture Absinthe made to the tent flap made it clear who they meant, "understand. I have been called all matter of things. He. She. They It. Thing from a few particularly nasty people."

"But you do not call yourself those." Especially not It. Alnyx couldn't fathom the walking Peacock using that.

"No, not really."

"So, what should I use?"

Silence fell for a moment after Alnyx asked again, and Absinthe's grin faltered as they looked anywhere but at the elf. Like they weren't sure what answer to give. After giving it a thought, the crooked grin returned.

"Just Absinthe." They echoed the elf's words from their first meeting, raising their eyes.

"Just Absinthe." Alnyx held their gaze for a moment before picking the glove up and going back to the stitching.

Alnyx very much could feel he was being watched. Staring. Searching for something. But he didn't look back. Finally there was the rustling of papers, the sound of them being shuffled together and piled up. From the corner of his eye, he could see the not so neat stack get set on the floor, and could hear when the worn cot moved as Absinthe lay down properly.

"Good night, Just Alnyx."

"Good night, Just Absinthe."

* * *

The camp was up with the sun, which meant the two of them were expected to be as well. Three really, but beyond a good full body shake and stretch, Fish required no time to get ready. Not like Absinthe apparently did. He hadn't noticed it the night on the road, likely because he had more packing up to do than a night in a borrowed tent required. Every step and movement were labored, as if Absinthe was moving through waist-deep water. Alnyx couldn't see how this zombie nearly burned someone to death like Cinna had said back at the Snakehead.

"We will set off after the morning meal. With any luck, we can be back here within a day or so."

Absinthe answered with a grunt, combing their fingers through their hair only to have it fall right back into their half-closed eyes. Alnyx's chuckle earned him a rather pointed glare.

"And you mocked my lack of responses."

"Scholars are nocturnal. Early morning sun is bullshit."

"Are they now?"

"This one is. Now shut up. Your voice is too much."

Alnyx was certain no one had ever accused him of talking too much. He managed to choke down a second laugh as the typically graceful creature stumbled as they pulled their boots on.

"They better have tea."

"In a camp full of hunters?" Alnyx snorted."Black coffee with no sugar at best."

"And they call us heathens."

He was the third son of the Elder of the Wind Nomads. Bearer of his clan's Freedom and Pride. The watcher at his side blessed by a Priestess of Prophecy and Battle from the Giant tribes of the Northern Mountains. Alnyx felt almost physically nauseous when he noticed his heart rate quicken at the scowl on Absinthe's lips when they took a moment to tie their hair back from their face.

He would be taking a break from the guild after this, he decided when Absinthe apparently finally felt presentable enough to walk from the tent. No more partnered cases. No risk of this sort of distraction. He would already have to work to focus on the hunt today. Distractions like this were deadly.

Tall. Svelte. A terrible morning person. And deadly.

4

Chapter 4

The difficult trek through the woods was exactly what Alnyx needed to focus on; anything that wasn't the the leggy scholar. The uneven ground and constant potential to run into either a low-hanging branch or a monstrous beast meant he couldn't even spare a glance in their direction. Scouting for tracks and listening for movement outside of their own left no time for empty chatter either.

"The clearing we're coming up on is the one the trainee and master hunter were attacked in."

He had lost track of how long they had been walking for since their last break, a few hours at least judging by the shifting of the sunlight through the branches. The soft sound of Absinthe's voice nearly startled him. He pulled the folded map from his pocket and gave it a glance to confirm. Not that he didn't believe them. With one sharp whistle he called to Fish, who had taken to padding ahead to create a wider perimeter.

Alnyx hadn't even realized he wasn't speaking to the Lycine in the common tongue until he could feel Absinthe's eyes on him. Habit when it was just the two of them, and it was as close to a first language that Fish would have. The creature seemed to understand, even giving what looked to be a nod of their fluffy head before briefly settling at the elf's feet.

"Rawan. My clan's native tongue." He answered the question before Absinthe could ask it.

"It's lovely."

They may have said something else after, but the elf turned his head sharply towards the opening in the trees not far ahead of them. It wasn't so much as a sight or a sound that pulled his attention. A feeling, of something bleak and dark.

"There."

An elk, black as pitch, stood a few meters in front of them near the clearing's center. From hoof to horn, it was more shadow than flesh and bone. It rippled like water, bending towards the stream to lap some into a mouth that did not open. The closest thing that Alnyx could think to compare it to in size was the giant moose that lived in the mountains, and it dwarfed even the largest of those that the had seen.

Even this brief glance was enough to know it would be foolish to try and take it by surprise with no plan. Slowly, Alnyx began to take steps backwards, not taking his eyes off the creature. Absinthe was quick to follow the elf's lead, while Fish lay still on the ground with his ears pointed in the beast's direction. The two of them continued to step backwards until the treeline swallowed their shape and Fish was only a dot of white among the leaf litter.

"What now?" Absinthe leaned on one of the nearest tree trunks, seeming short of breath but managing to keep themselves calm.

"Fish will track it to its den. We follow him." Alnyx explained, walking to a nearby fallen log ans sitting on it and stretching his legs out in front of him as he did. "You said yesterday that it will be vulnerable in whatever its natural state is."

"In theory, yes" Absinthe nodded. "I've never seen one in the wild. Normally, the territory of these sorts of things are closer to rifts or exposed parts of lines. Neither of those are anywhere near here based on the most recent charts the scholars have of the area."

"The closest rift is still the one that started in the marshes?" Alnyx asked which got him another nod. "Several days. It shouldn't have been able to get this far unnoticed until now."

"Honestly? My best guess is a local scholar. A....pet or a toy that ran away from a master." the word didn't seem to sit well with Alnyx, and it clearly showed on his face judging by Absinthe's quick follow up. "An experiment. Shifters like that and their parts have many uses in ritual magic and alchemy."

"Their parts."

"It isn't always pretty work like smokeless fires and reading books." They shrugged. "But yes. Probably why it was hostile when a human got too close, mage or not. If it was being used for experiments, it would only associate them with pain and fear. Probably panicked. They aren't... Advanced enough to have complex feelings and thoughts. If Fish, for example, is like a teenager because he can understand you somewhat and take orders when he wants, the ley beasts are toddlers."

Alnyx wouldn't say he fully understood, but the analogy was easy enough to follow. He let out a "hmm" of a grunt before taking the small travel pack off his back. He offered up a chunk of hardened bread from it, which Absinthe took and sat beside him on the nearest fallen log. The way they wrinkled their nose said the dry, crumbly texture disturbed them. But, hunger won out.

"This is the sort of thing you study then? Creatures and their...parts?"

"No. Not directly I mean." they wiped crumbs off of their fingers with a chuckle. "Ingredients and how they're obtained is sort of like...How I imagine you know if that mushroom over there is poisonous or good to eat. Things you pick up as a part of the job."

That part Alnyx could understand. When you hunted as a way of life in the way his people were used to, you knew how to use every part of a kill. Guts for this, skin for that. Fussy an impractical as they liked to look, Scholars and magic had to be at least somewhat resourceful.

"How are you going to find Fish? I imagine that he's going to be able to duck and get around better than the two of us. Even if he's white as freshly bleached linen."

"He is my Watcher, and I am his Guide. We know where one another is at all times."

"The more you speak, the less I know. You'll have to explain that to me some time."

"Perhaps."

They settled back into silence as they ate their miserable excuse for a midday meal, getting what rest they could. Having caught sight of the beast, they would have to move quickly to avoid losing it. After re-securing his pack again once he determined it had been long enough, Alnyx stood and headed back off toward the clearing. Absinthe groaned before scrambling after him.

There was no sign of the beast left, or of Fish. As they stood beside the stream, there were a confused mess of hoof prints and other markings from the native beasts. Absinthe couldn't make heads or tails of any of it. Alnyx let him try to puzzle it out before he pointed to one spot on the ground.

A single, near perfect, impression of the lycine's paw pad. The toes seemed to point to the north east, where there was a freshly broken tree limb.

"Damn clever beast isn't he." The mage chuckled, clearly impressed.

"He likes to think so."

* * *

Absinthe and Alnyx kept a healthy distance between themselves and the two beasts. A paw print here, a claw mark on a tree there: it was clear this wasn't the first time Lycine and Elf had worked this way. If the silence wasn't absolutely necessary, Absinthe might have even made further mention of how impressive it was.

As they ventured deeper and deeper into the Kingswood, it grew darker more quickly than was natural. Even with the dense canopy of the trees, some light should have broken through. The limited sight slowed them to a crawl, almost a stop, until the horned mage used a bit of magic to create a smokeless light source, this time with a palm-sized rock, a pinch of moss from one of the trees, and a few words Alnyx didn't even pretend to understand.

Something was off, both of them were certain. There wasn't any sign of animals, outside the markings they were following. The birdsong from earlier in the wood was long since silent, and even the insects seemed to stop flying at their faces. The stillness of the air was heavy, abrasive. Like dragging a hand the wrong way across velvet, Absinthe thought to themselves.

"A moment." They put a hand on Alnyx's arm to stop him from moving forward. "I have to....Not a break, don't look at me like that. There is something I have to do."

"There are plenty of trees to go behind."

"Trees...Oh no, not that!" They were glad the dim light from their spelled stone wouldn't give enough for the elf to see the color that rose to their cheeks. "A magic thing. You may not be able to use the lines yourself, but even you can feel it.."

Alnyx's grunt was as close to agreement that They would get. The elf scanned across the area, to find somewhere they wouldn't lose the trail, but also wouldn't be directly in the open should the beast be closer than the last few markings said. He pointed to a few large rocks and the remnants of a broken and cracked tree trunk nearby. A flat enough surface for whatever the mage might need, and coverage to duck behind.

"Ah, perfectly serviceable. Good eye." Absinthe patted Alnyx's shoulder and removed the pack from their back. "It may be nothing.

If the beast has been here for as long as the camp's reporting makes it seem, it may be residual energy from it rubbing up on everything."

"But it may not be nothing." A statement, not a question. The rumors of the so called "wild elves" being more brawn than brain Absinthe heard from the LeyKissed of the tower were being proven more false every time Alnyx spoke. Blessings on blessings.

"Precisely. Could be whatever brought it to this specific Wood." They set their bag down on the hip-high stump and began to dig through it. "Better to be safe than to be sorry."

Another grunt of a response, and the horned mage looked over at Alnyx. The elf stood a short distance away, one hand ever resting on the hilt of a blade. He watched, not with the curiosity or awe that some did when mages prepared reagents, but with caution. Alnyx knew enough about Scholars and the way their mages were taught to not trust it entirely.

Good. Absinthe thought before going back to their bag. *Silent distrust is easier than when people hover.*

"I'm going to see if I can determine what is around us, if that makes sense." The silence said it didn't, so they went on. "Different sorts of power will leave different impressions. Like the paw prints Fish is leaving for us. In a place as old as this, I would expect the trees themselves, obviously my own magic and something from the beast as well. So, I'm looking for an outlier. Something that doesn't belong."

It wasn't clear if explaining it made things better or worse. But, it seemed to be a good enough, as Alnyx turned his back to keep watch on the woods instead of Absinthe. Enough trust that the mage wasn't going to do anything to directly get them killed.

A gray feather, a piece of clear quartz, and a pinch of the dry soil under them. Pausing for a moment, they broke a piece of the bark from the trunk for good measure, setting the stone and feather on top of it. Absinthe sprinkled the soil over it and spoke words in a tongue nearly as old as the trees of the Kingswood. There was a warming, and a pulse of energy surely even Alnyx would feel from the horned mage's chest. The feeling of a spell properly taking hold and work done well never failed to cause Absinthe's breath to hitch for just a moment, even benign ones like this. They used the feather to clean the dust from the quartz before lifting it, top and bottom points of the crystal between thumb and middle finger. Where the stone was once clear, there were now distinct bands of color across the the largest facet of the prism.

Their own, acid green to match their eyes and veins. Black, the beast that they were tracking. Brown, the bark of the ancient wood. A tiny strip of blue, which nearly startled them. Until they realized it was the very same blue of Fish's eyes. A stripe of color ran perpendicular to all the others, and was a violet. It was frayed, feathered and branching out from the one solid line.

"There is a fissure here." Absinthe sighed, shaking the crystal back and forth a few times. "An offshoot from one of the main lines most likely. Small enough to not have to be cataloged or dormant until out shape-shifting troublemaker showed up, if I were the betting sort."

"Is that a problem?"

"Could be. Not one for us, though." They tucked the crystal and feather back into their pack, kneeling on the ground and digging a small hole in the dirt. "I'll report it to the Alabaster Square when we get back. They'll send someone out to investigate further. It just may make killing the thing more....Difficult even inside a den."

"That seems like a problem then."

"If it's been feeding off of an exposed line, it's going to have a greater physical strength. Faster too. But, we're still smarter and more capable." the piece of bark that served as a tray for the spell went into the hole, and they covered it with a quiet prayer of thanks and a handful of the dirt.

"Don't suppose you could just...take us to it?"

"The spell doesn't work like that, no. I can tell the whats, but not the where." Absinthe stood, brushing the remaining dirt from their hands and putting their pack back over their shoulders. "For anything like travel, I'd have to have another scholar with me. Or be touching the line directly. And with a broken one-"

"I got it." Alnyx shook their head, not caring about the why. "Let's move. We're nearly out of the light we do have left."

Absinthe gestured back towards the path in a clear "lead the way", the glowing rock still providing light floating above their other hand that was outstretched with palm skyward. While they trusted Alnyx's abilities to do what it is he was hired to do, a broken leyline this close to a settlement should have been noticed. As if he could sense the desire to not linger, Alnyx picked up the pace as they followed the freshest print they had seen.

5

Chapter 5

Even without the tracks, the path the creature took became more obvious once they broke through the obscuring tree line and had natural light once more. The ground-cover plants were brown and dead. Rot crept up the trunks of the ancient trees, spreading to the branches. Some of them had snapped and fallen, reaching up from the ground like skeletal limbs from a grave.

"All from the beast?" Alnyx wrinkled his nose, bending down and breaking off a part of one of the branches, which turned to ash in his fingers.

"No, no shape shifting beast could do this. The fissure must have been...Corrupted by something, so it started to leak."

"This is still not our problem?"

"At least not the one we're being paid for." They raised their hand to wrap around the floating stone, the light growing dark as they could use what was still left of the sun once more. "If it's all the same, I'd like to make this quick. The sooner the Scholars-"

They heard Fish before they saw him. A brief, low, growl of warning. The elf drew his blades in an instant as the flash of white broke from the decaying trees and cracks rocks. The dark shape that followed it was no longer an elk. It wasn't…,.Anything at all.

Aspic was the only was Alnyx could think to describe it. A mountain giant-sized, undulating, pile of aspic moving right towards them. It had tentacles made of the stuff, one of which was thick as a tree trunk as it swiped out towards the three of them, only barely missing as they scattered. Every branch and remnant of tree it struck splintered with deafening cracks as it cut through them.

"You said it would be weaker in its den!"

"Before I knew we were dealing with a potentially corrupted leyline on top of everything, thank you!" Absinthe raised both of their hands, bending and contorting their fingers until acid green energy danced between them like spiderwebs.

"What are we meant to do then?"

Alnyx was able to cleave one of his twin blades through another pseudo-pod that came at him. It fell with a noisy splat to the ground. After a moment it began to twitch and move back towards the largest part of the mass.

"Absinthe!"

"Yes I can see, give me a moment to think!" A wave of their hand, so the tendril that made its way towards them hit only a wall of light and burned away.

Fish was wise to get closer to Absinthe while the mage tried to figure out a plan. Every tentacle that burned or was cut away seemed to grow three more in its place. Whatever fool let this thing get out of its lab infused the blood of a hydra into it before it got away.

"There should be a center mass. A core. You know, like a heart I guess?"

"I need something more than a guess!"

"I'm not exactly used to planning while being attacked! Look for something solid inside of it. Or…More solid I guess."

"Stop saying that!"

It wasn't clear if the growl came from Alnyx or Fish. But when a tendril was missed by Absinthe's flame, the Lycine pounced and ripped into it with his jaws. Were the beast a natural wolf, it would have squished through like jelly. Instead, the air around Fish seemed to smoke, coming more concentrated from its partially open maw. The way your breath was visible in the cold. The pseudopod it kept pinned with fang and claw began to ice over, bursting to shards when the jaw tightened and snapped it off.

"Such a brilliant boy aren't you?" Absinthe couldn't help but be at least a little impressed, looking back in Alnyx's direction.

The elf had been trying to move closer to the thing, with some success. He bent backwards as one of the tendrils shot out directly towards his chest, grunting at the strain it put on his back before being able to straighten as it went back the way it came. Spikes of it came up from the ground as he got closer. It was aware enough to know which of them was the larger danger at the moment.

"Can you see it yet?" Absinthe called.

"There are lots of solid things in it." Bones, trees, rocks. One of the skulls that floated by was decidedly humanoid. "How am I supposed to know what it is and what it isn't?"

"Look for the outliers!"

"What does that even MEAN?!" The last word was half word and half pained gasp, as the momentary distraction allowed the shapeshifter to get one of the thick tentacles around his middle.

Alnyx was certain he could feel his ribs cracking under the band of both solid and not solid goo. With some maneuvering, he managed to get his sword through the tentacle, severing it from the whole. He fell onto his knees, head bent to catch his breath. Bracing himself for a hit that didn't come when a howl erupted on his left, Fish to the rescue.

"Alnyx are you–"

"I'm fine. Stay back." The elf pulled himself back to his feet before

Absinthe could move forward. "Stay back. I'll find the damned heart."

"Outlier!"

"That still means nothing!"

With the Lycine closer, able to help deflect and distract, Alnyx was able to take better stock of the creature. The mass of aspic wriggled and rippled, every bit of it seeming to be in constant motion. Even the center parts of it, which seemed to generate the endless psudeopods, never seemed to be quite stable. He was certain if he reached out a hand to touch it, he'd feel it vibrate.

An outlier. This whole ancestor-cursed thing is an outlier. He kept the thought to himself. *No brain, no lungs, and sure as The Grove itself no heart.*

Not from where he was sitting anyway. Sitting....Wait, that was it. Organs. Organs didn't move. Something had to center it enough for its limited thought. So, what WASN'T moving?

Judging from the heavy panting from Fish, and the way the flashes of flame seemed less and less bright, he didn't have much time to figure it out. Ducking under another spear of aspic, he got within an arm's reach of the center, and kept moving around it. He couldn't stay still long enough to get more than glances. The thing had no chitin, no armor, and couldn't create a spike that would pierce his flesh. But he didn't want to test the speed at which the blunt tendrils came out in case they could force their way through.

Finally, after what felt like an eternity, he spotted a form within that didn't seem to move as everything around it did. Near the "top" of the center of the mass. More brain than heart.

"Got you, bastard."

Whatever energy he had left, he mustered into the leap upwards, one sword dropped on the ground and the other in both hands over his head. As he brought it down, through the thick layer of aspic and finally made contact with the solid mass, it was difficult to cut through. The sword got stuck just an inch into it, the whole mass thrashing violently, like it was trying to dislodge him. Alnyx had to put his whole body wight into the push, sinking inch by agonizing inch until the mass was cleaved in two.

As if it being whole was the only thing keeping the whole of the massive thing sentient and fighting, and perhaps it was, the movement stopped. Almost instantly, the aspic became liquid, like ice melting. And with nothing to keep Alnyx or the mass upright, they tumbled to the ground. The stone-like center twitched, a squeal of a noise coming from it like a cry. As if it had eyes to see the elf pulling the dagger from his belt, and was begging to be spared.

Alnyx's hand made contact with the sopping wet mass as he brought the dagger through it to silence the noise. Pain. Rage. Sorrow. The feelings hit him all at once, being passed through the skin to not skin contact.

"Who is really the monster here?" it said without words. Alnyx left the blade in as he pulled himself to his feet.

The way he brought his booted foot down on it, effectively ending the noise, answered the unspoken question.

Fish's giant, furry head against his thigh was grounding as it always was as the Lycine came to him. Both of them were coated in the cooling now liquid of what had been the body. Fish extracted the dagger by the handle with his teeth and offered it up. Back into its sheath it went.

"Are....You all right?" Absinthe's voice was soft. Hesitant. Like they didn't think they were meant to see the way Alnyx had to lean Fish for support to keep his feet under him. "That was...Something else."

Battered, bruised, likely a broken rib at the very least. Alnyx was far from all right. But there was such sincerity in the question, that he couldn't bring himself to be snappy. So he simply grunted.

" 'lmake it." Not a yes or no. "We need to bring back proof for the contract."

"I can handle that. You...You should probably sit down or something."

They set their pack on the ground, digging through it for something.

Alnyx didn't need to be told twice. He dragged himself to one of the tree trunks that had been knocked down, leaning against it. Sore as everything felt, the weight of Fish's head on his lap and the way he nuzzled into his legs kept his mind from it.

And so did watching the precise way that Absinthe worked. The liquid would just look like water to the unknowing eye, but some of it went into a jar before it was too soaked into the dirt and mud. Tainted it wouldn't be as potent an ingredient. But everything had a use. Into the bag the jar went after it was cleaned off with a handkerchief that was far too nice a material for what it was being put through.

Absinthe stepped to the remnants of the "heart" as they had called it, head tilting one way and the other as they sized it up. Back to the pack, they pulled out two boxes that seemed too large to be able to fit into the rigid leather. One half went into each, and they went in with the jar.

"Did you...."

"A good scholar is always prepared for whatever may come." Absinthe winked, and then picked up the elf's sword that had been left on the ground. "Half should be more than enough for a trophy for the Taskers I think."

Alnyx didn't have the energy to argue. He watched as Absinthe cleaned his blades off with the fine cloth and walk towards him to hand them back over. They'd have to be properly cleaned of what was left of the beast. Judging by the audible gag Fish gave when he tried to lick some of the mess from his fur, the metal wasn't the only thing in need of some sort of fresh water.

* * *

Absinthe led the way this time, as Alnyx took time to sheath the blades and still leaned on Fish for shared strength as they made their way out of the dead vegetation and back to the green of the Kingswood. Even if the elf was able to travel at the speed he had on the way in, it was too dark for them to make their way back to the Huntsmen camp tonight. So, they found a suitable clearing, and Absinthe went about setting out sleeping rolls.

"You're hurt." They said, as if it wasn't obvious in the way Alnyx was clearly breathing irregularly and moving exactly as much as necessary.

"It's fine. A few bruises. Usual for most Taskers."

"Bullshit, Let me look at you."

"There's nothing for you to see."

It certainly wasn't because Alnyx wasn't sure he could get his tunic off on his own, let alone unlaced. Of course not. He even managed to contain a wince when he tried to take off his sword belt so he could sit in a more comfortable way.

"Don't play hero. It isn't a good look for you." And neither was the way Absinthe's brows knit together and caused wrinkles when they said it. "Let me look. Where does it hurt?"

Everywhere didn't seem to be an appropriate answer for the moment. And the fact that even the not at all painful shake of his head didn't deter them said Alnyx wasn't going to be able to continue getting away with non answers.

"Ribs. The thing had a tighter grip than I thought. I don't feel any true breaks." He didn't say anything about fractures though. "It's fine."

He tried to lean away when Absinthe, who had sat close by once the light source was set, reached out their hand to touch him. He only managed to aggravate the pain, letting out a hiss of pain.

"That isn't fine. Shirt off, or I'm going to take it off for you."

Alnyx hated the brief image the phrasing gave him. Not the time, not the place. No matter how-

"Come on now. I need you in one piece to collect this coin. I don't need Marigold thinking I was feeling greedy."

The contract. Of course. The horned scholar was going to need to make sure He lived since his name was the primary on the contract in order to get paid in any sort of decent time. Investigations and suspending payments in suspicious circumstances weren't unheard of.

"Fine." Alnyx tried to go for annoyance with the growl, but it quickly became more of a pained sound when hands were laid on him.

He was little help as Absinthe worked the laces out of the leather armor, snarling at every pull and bit of pressure. It was clear that they were trying to be delicate, but the rawhide strings seemed to get caught in every single eyelet on both sides. Finally, all that was left was to get it over his head. The elf shook his head once it came up and over, as the head hole side knocked against his ears.

"Oh you poor thing. Those look terrible."

A thick band of deep colored bruising two hands wide all the way around his torso at his ribs. No broken skin, since the pseudopods hadn't really been capable of it. And if there were breaks, that meant they stayed inside. Alnyx wasn't sure if that made him feel better or worse. And now, Absinthe would be able to see all the scars a decade of working for the Taskers earned. Claws and teeth here. A blade from a foolish cultist there. Burns and pockmarked skin from mages whose powers never agreed with him. In some spots, it was as if he was more scar tissue than not.

"May I?" Absinthe asked more as a warning before their hands touched the bare ribs.

Their hands radiated warmth, and weren't as soft as Alnyx expected them to be. Scholars, healers, academics; they all had hands like noblemen in his experience. They didn't do the kind of work that would allow callouses to form. Perhaps the flames they used came at a price.

"You might be right about the breaks. I can't be sure though, not without a probing examination I don't have the training or tools for. Any numbness or tingling of any kind?"

"Told you 'mfine." He snorted. "Didn't take you for a healer."

"I know enough to keep myself alive. Can you picture me at some poor bastard's bedside? They'd assume they already died and were in the Hells."

Alnyx wanted to laugh with Them, but even the thought of the action hurt too much, so it was mostly a huff of air. The wrinkle of Absinthe's nose said they understood it for what it was. Already. The fact that Alnyx could get used to the mage being there wasn't a welcome one. He was going to have to have a talk with Marigold about trying to set him up. He had assumed that punishment for gently rebuffing her advances would get him someone incompetent. Not the girl playing Cupid.

"Did you hear me?"

Alnyx blinked, answer enough for Absinthe as they shook their head.

"I asked if you carry and balms or salves with you for these sorts of things."

"For bruises and a little bit of pain?" Alnyx scoffed. "No. They're just bruises. Not all of us have bags that apparently are portals to never-ending storage spaces."

"You don't travel with the right sorts then. I'll see what I have."

He found himself briefly mourning the warmth of the hands. Instead, he went back to focusing on the constant pressure of Fish sprawled across his legs. A soothing weight. He closed his eyes, resting his head back against the tree he had sat under.

"Here we are. Probably not enough for more than the trip back with how big it is...."

Alnyx kept his eyes closed as Absinthe returned to his side. With just a turn of the lid of whatever they brought with, he was assaulted with a pungent odor. He could smell it even with with drying aspic and ichor on his skin. Even Fish lifted his head.

"I get it from one of the herbalists I work with. Little more...Potent stuff than you can pick up for sale at the markets."

"It smells like a fertilizer heap." When Absinthe laughed, he peaked his eyes back open. "What? It does."

"You're no prairie rose yourself at the moment you know." They shook their head. "It'll help so you can sleep without pain and hopefully prime some of the healing work. If you can't move in the morning, I'm not going to be able to carry you."

"Fish can. Has."

"By the Weave you're absurd."

There was no gentle warning when they touched him this time. And the warmth was replaced with an icy chill. Apparently the pocket of space the inside of the bag inhabited was freezing. It didn't help that it also stung something terrible when Absinthe began to smooth it over his skin. He couldn't help the pained groan.

"You were more quiet when it was trying to kill you." Absinthe had no pity for him. "Echinacea. It works as a numbing agent along with all the bits that help with healing. The tingle means it's working."

"You were right. You would make a terrible healer."

"Oi!" the smack to his shoulder was accompanied by an equally sharp laugh. "Don't insult your healer, or the person preparing your food. Important rules."

"Good thing I haven't asked you to cook for me then."

"Keep it up and I'll take the balm back."

"No." he winced at the desperation in his answer. Didn't want to let on just how much the tingling salve was helping.

"That's what I thought. Now, hold still and let me finish."

6

Chapter 6

Alnyx didn't sleep particularly well that night. With the injuries that was hardly a surprise, but it made his usual rising with the sun that much more difficult. He winced when he pulled himself up from the sleeping roll and the ground, but it wasn't as bad as it might have been. His entire torso felt disgustingly sticky from the balm, and the residue clung to him worse than the dried gelatinous mess from the beast. No sense in getting the other set of clothes he'd thrown in his bag dirty, so he pulled yesterday's shirt on.

Fish had been using it as a pillow, giving a tired little whine when it was tugged from under his giant, furry, head. Seeing the elf clearly getting ready to go, the Lycine got onto its own legs, stretching ans shaking itself out with a yawn that showed those sharp teeth.

"Sooner we get moving, the sooner we're out of these woods and can get finished." Alnyx scratched behind Fish's ear briefly. "We can't let Them sleep in much longer...

He had to admit, he was hesitant to jostle Absinthe and not just because of the story the barman had told about getting set on fire. Using ley powers took energy, no matter how good you might have been at it. How much of themselves had they burned on those beams and shields? Alnyx

48

couldn't be sure. Just one other unsettling way that the horned mage was new territory.

The normally glowing lines of acid green were dimmer when they slept, like the embers of a flame that had spend the whole night burning. Alnyx hadn't noticed that before. Though he hadn't really been looking.

Not that Absinthe looked "normal" even in rest. The charcoal gray skin coupled with the horns saw to that. They had tossed and turned in their sleep, so the blanket was barely covering them anymore. They slept fully clothed, save the boots. Used to being ready, it was admirable. Alnyx couldn't help but notice the sheath for the boot blade was empty, though. Under the pillow, perhaps?

"I can feel you staring. 'm up." And yet, Absinthe's eyes did not open yet as they mumbled. "You would be a terrible spy."

"Good morning to you too." Alnyx turned quickly away, before Absinthe could open their eyes and risk seeing the brief flush of color. "Since you're up, we can get going. I want to be back at the Huntsman camp before dark."

"Mmhmm, not THAT up." Absinthe hid their face in their pack which had been doubling as a pillow. "Wake me in another bell."

"I will be leaving in fifteen."

"Fifteen?"

"Fourteen. Thirteen."

"You wouldn't dare."

"Twelve. Eleven."

"Bloody monster of a thing aren't you." The groan as their eyes opened and they sat up was more than a little exaggerated. "Happy?"

Their hair was ruffled from the rough sleep, a snowflake halo of knots and wisps. Rumpled and wrinkled like this they were...So far from the imposing air they normally carried. Especially when they let out a squeak of a yawn and rubbed their eyes with the heels of their palms.

"Am I the one that almost broke ribs yesterday, or you?" Alnyx arched an eyebrow. "You would think I was asking you to fight another beast."

"Nocturnal." they groaned, back popping as they stretched before finally dragging themselves to their feet. "Sun's bullshit."

"Which you are full of. I would think you'd get on."

"I think I prefer your grunts. Too early for wit." They pulled a comb from their bag to address the knots. "What time even is it?"

"Not long since dawn. We have plenty of daylight."

"Why on EARTH did you wake me then?" They glared, pointing the implement like a weapon. "You're a masochist. That's what it is, isn't it? You enjoy seeing good, innocent, weave-conscious people suffer."

"Ten. Nine."

A stare off. Which of them would blink first? Absinthe's impossible smirk against Alnyx's perfectly neutral face.

"Eight. Seven." A pause. "Six. Five. Four-"

A crashing of branches from somewhere nearby had Fish instantly on alert. Hackles raise and growling. Alnyx turned his head in the same direction. He crouched, hand on the hilt of a blade, ready to move if needed.

"Absinthe."

"Fine." the mage huffed, shoving the comb back into their bag before starting to tug their boots on. "The fact you are a masochist still stands."

Absinthe grumbled the entire time they packed both their own things and Alnyx's, so the elf could be ready in case there was something that they had missed and would need to defend against. And while it had only been a boar that got too close, it really was best they head out as soon as they were able.

The group of three stopped in the clearing with the stream running through it by midday to refill water canteens and do at least a cursory sort of cleaning. Alnyx was going to need much more than dabbing with a damp cloth and a splashing of water against his skin. At least getting some of the worse bits off seemed to put Absinthe in a better mood. They even offered to use what was left the balm on Alnyx's ribs.

"I trust you can deliver the report to Bennett?" the elf asked, managing not to wince at the stinging of the balm this time. "You'll explain it better."

"So long as you take the time to go to the healer tent." Absinthe insisted, but it was clear they weren't sure Alnyx actually would. "Yes, that's fine."

As they made their was to the camp, before the sun fell thanks to their quick pace, Alnyx could not help but pause at the crossroad between the Hunstmaster's tent and the medical one. It felt...Strange. Parting even briefly from Absinthe. They hadn't been apart since they had met at the Snakehead Inn for any real stretch. Less than a week, but the presence of someone besides Fish being in arms reach had become normal feeling. Natural. Almost as if–

"Well, I'll come make sure the healers have had their way with you once I give our report." Absinthe's words shook him from his thoughts, coupled with a nudge to the back of the knee from Fish.

Alnyx gave no words in response, just a nod. The feel of fur under his fingers was comforting as he and the lycine walked towards the healer's tent. They both seemed to be stepping a little slower and more tenderly than they might normally.

"I know. I know." Alnyx spoke soft enough so only Fish would hear him. "Once we receive our pay, we'll go see the Family. Before the weather turns. You'd like that, wouldn't you?"

The thump of a tail against his leg and the snort was an agreement. Smiling, they made their way past the tent flap.

* * *

Huntsmaster Bennet had been more than happy to provide his seal to the contract once Absinthe laid out the whole of the tale for him. Combining it with the exposed, fractured leyline, and the urgency that would be needed to address it, there was no questioning their thorough work. Barrett was more than happy to give them the tent for the night again, as well as another meal. Combined with a healer he didn't have to pay for, Alnyx was certain that it had to be the mot successful job he had taken in recent memory.

Thanks to the kindness of the night's rest, they were able to move at their full pace, with only minimal winging from his injuries. Blissfully, there were no interruptions on the road. Not even a trader of any kind. They settled for the night near the same site they had used leaving the port.

"Do you stay in town, then? I've heard the Taskers talking about the housing the guild provides for a cut of profit."

There wasn't any game about, so it was dried trail rations for supper. They had been able to heat some water to make the oats and berries a little more palatable at least. The metal of Absinthe's spoon clanked against their cup as they asked the question.

"No. I work along the highroads. When the weather turns, I will go south with the last of the caravans to make sure work stays steady."

"The Highroads, ey? A traveling man. Suits you."Absinthe chuckled, setting the cup down to dig a flask from their bag. "A thief? Or an escort?"

"Depends on what is paying better." Alnyx deadpanned, shaking his head when Absinthe held the flask over in an offering. "Typically the second one."

"Makes sense why I couldn't recognize you. I know almost all the resident Taskers at the port." They took a deep swig, wiping off their mouth on the back of their hand. "We're still a bit out from the weather turning though."

"Business along the roads slowed down a moon ago. Early this year." Alnyx shrugged, patting Fish's side when the beast curled closer to him.

"Likely, I'll go and visit my clan in the north. So long as I can get out before the snows come. This partner work is....Not exactly my style."

"Oh you rude thing, I'm sitting right here." Absinthe gasped in mock offense but it was followed by a laugh. "You've a fair point. I wouldn't worry too much. They already arrested the fool anyway."

"Did they?"

"Mmmhm. Only a few days before we left." Another swig and the flask was capped and slipped away. "He'll likely hang. The price you pay for thinking with your...Southern head though, isn't it? Attraction to the target can get messy."

It hit too close to home for Alnyx. He didn't answer, shifting so he lay on his back instead. Fish used his chest as a pillow, making it so he could do little else but look skyward. And yet, he felt Absinthe's eyes linger on him.

"Good night, Alnyx."

"Good night, Absinthe."

7

Chapter 7

"Well, The Divines are shining on me today. My three favorites returned to me, and all in one piece."

"Marigold, my dear cherub. Do you ever take a day off? The chair behind that desk must be imprinted with the shape of you. The envy of all the stools in the Greater Kingdoms."

"Flattery doesn't get you extra coin." and yet she batted her lashes at Absinthe. "My Fishy Fish. Precious, perfect, lad." She stepped form behind the counter and knelt to cup the beast's head and give him pets. "And Alnyx of course."

"Marigold." the elf grunted in acknowledgment. "The contract's done."

"Not a social visit then?" she made sure Fish was already chomping on the jerky she had snuck him before standing. "I didn't expect you for at least a few more days, based on the original report."

"I demanded we hurry back. Haven't had proper bedding in days and it's put me in a mood." Absinthe's dramatic sigh had Marigold giggling.

"Kingswood seal is already on the paperwork." Alnyx tried to speed things along.

"Timely and thorough. Knew I was right to hand things over to you."

"Only the best for the royals of the content." Absinthe preened and leaned on the counter as Marigold went back behind it.

"Your modesty is always unmatched." she held her hand out for the contract that Alnyx had started to pull out. "Let's see....Good, looks to be in order. Let's see if they have the coin split out for you."

She disappeared as she knelt behind the high desk, to what had to be the safe they kept payments in, just the top of her curly hair visible. The groan said that things had very much not been split.

"That's what I get for letting the night shift kid do anything." she straightened herself back out, bag of coin clinking at her side as she pulled it out. "Lemme run to the back right quick and get it counted out for you."

The two muttered an agreed "all right" as Marigold went through a door behind her. Alnyx leaned one hip against the desk, turned so he was facing Absinthe.

"Are you local? The Snakehead isn't exactly cheap."

"No, it isn't." they agreed with a laugh. "I'm based further North, around the curve of the bay. The Alabaster Square's central School. I came down this way to assist on a more....Delicate project. My last day in town was meant to be the day you found me, actually."

"Fortunate."

"Mmhm. Some might even say there was a touch of destiny about it." Their laugh said what they thought of destiny. "I've been down here more and more as of late. They may just have me temporarily base here. They think moving me would be cheaper than paying my room and tab. Until they see the scope of my closet and bookshelves."

"I wouldn't have pegged you as being from that area. The people that stay close to the places the Alabaster are. They're...."

"Uptight and outright assholes? Sticks up their asses and their noses high enough up they'll drown in the rain? They are, you're absolutely right. But, one of the better cities for freaks like me." Alnyx's arched eyebrow made them go on. "The horns scare most people, even here. There, the University's presence and the Embassies for some of the Species make it a little easier."

"Hmm."

"They probably wouldn't even balk at Fish. Even though he smells like wet cabbage." the lycine let out a whine-growl as if they understood. "Wet dog is one thing. You, my wintry friend, have transcended that."

Fish allowed Absinthe to touch him. Not even just a pet or a pat. A poke to the tip of the nose. And the snap and turn of the head was more...In play than in annoyance. It was all the mage got before the beast turned its back on the both of them any lay back down.

"Here we are! Even down the middle minus all fees." Marigold returned with two small bags this time, setting them on the counter with a plop. "The extra small coins went to Fishy."

"I suppose things would have been much more difficult if we didn't have him tracking." Absinthe picked up the bag closest to them, weighing it in their hand. "I do love a noble contract. They pay in the good stuff."

They fished out a square piece of platinum and tapped it against the desktop, as if having to test it was real. Alnyx took the other bag, tying it to his belt for now. His fingers stumbled over the knot when the sound of a throat clearing was clearly meant to get his attention.

"This was fun. Minus the fact I'll have to burn the clothes that got all that goo on them." Absinthe smiled when their eyes met. "Look me up the next time you're in town. Or near the Square. We'll do this again."

Before Alnyx could say that he absolutely would not be doing so, they walked away. The click of their heels against the floor was what kept Alnyx's attention on them until the door open and closed. Or at least that was what he would say.

"Well? What did you think? He's pretty cool, right?" Marigold bounced on her heels. "For a bookworm anyway. I knew you two would get on!"

"Marigold."

"And that line? Look me up the next time you're in town." she poorly mimicked Absinthe's voice. "I mean, come on."

"Mari–"

"In fact, I've got the perf–"

"Marigold, enough." He didn't like to raise his voice, but she hadn't given him an option. "Absinthe was fine. Competent. All right?"

"Fine? Just fine?" she frowned. "I guess I could...Find someone else for another task for you. You kinda scare the regulars with all that scowling you do."

"No, Marigold. I don't need you to set me up." he paused a little too long before adding "With a partner for contracts. The headache isn't worth the cut in pay. I'll be taking a break, until things normalize."

She huffed and crossed her arms at him. Sometimes, Alnyx forgot that she was young, even by human standards. She leaned on the counter, pile of contracts pushed over to one side so she could lean her elbow on it after a moment with her chin on her hand.

"What are you gonna do if you aren't working? It isn't even cold yet."

"I'll be going to the Grove. To see my clan. I am past due for a visit."

"Hmm. Well, bring me a present." she narrowed her eyes at him, in an attempt to seem serious. "Or else next time, you're going to get a job cleaning up some gross monster mess." The laugh meant her attempt failed.

"I will see you in a few moons, Marigold."

"Eight Divines keep you, Alnyx. You too, Fishy Fish."

He adjusted his bag before walking out, with the Lycine at his side. Yes, a few moons among his brothers and sisters would be good. And would force Marigold to find someone else to make her project.

* * *

Alnyx did not immediately leave town. The trip up north to The Grove would take more supplies than he normally carried, as there weren't many settlements to replenish for fair coin. And perhaps another night or two in a proper bed was a luxury the royal coin could allow. Fish certainly didn't seem to mind.

The inn he usually frequented when he stayed in town was a bed-share, above a tavern that was frequented by the dockworkers and day laborers across the city. They never turned their noses up if he came in dirty, baths were cheap, and the girls that ran the kitchen had a soft spot for his furry companion. Usually, it meant spending a little less on food those nights as they slipped Fish treats. He was currently chewing on a cattle bone as the elf sat on the bed, bundling up his supplies and making sure the whole of his mental list was checked off.

There was a decent amount of coin left. Thank the Ancestors for royals who couldn't figure out their own problems. Combined with being willing to take guard shifts, there would be enough for a spot on a caravan down south if proper work really had fully dried up by the time he was on his way back.

The Alabaster Square isn't too far. Just more to the west. Barely a day's detour. A quiet voice he tried his best to silence nudged. Because yes, It was very much on the way to The Grove with only a slight bend. But, he shook his head.

Alnyx gave the coins another count, putting aside what he knew he'd need for that last resort caravan spot. A tip for the folks that would turn the bed down in the morning. Just enough left for a drink. Or three.

"I'll be back in a few hours. Stay here. Cause no trouble."

Fish looked up from the floor, licking his lips. He left the bone on the floor for the moment and jumped onto the bed, nestling his head right into the pillows. Alnyx chuckled and patted his haunch.

"No trouble." he repeated and got one bark in response. "Good boy."

It was already a few hours past sundown. The tavern below the bed-share started to fill up, so it took him longer to get his way though the already half drunk packed crowd. It wasn't that it was a bad place to drink, but he kept his sleeping and his leisure separate. Besides, it was a nice night for a walk across the Merchant district.

The stalls and shops of any respectable nature were closed down for the night or in the process of it. A few coppers and he bought out the last two meat-pies at a bakery, seeing a few dirty half-elf children staring through the window. A pat on the head and telling them to head off home, got him a smile from the woman locking up the flower shop next door that he shrugged off before he continued on his way.

The Hatpin was originally the name of the tailor that had been the neighbor of the tavern, which was a failed haberdashery before that. Somewhere down the line, the tavern got too big, the old seamstress passed, and her grown children hadn't picked up her trade. They were more than happy to leave Morgranto for one of the larger cities with the coin the tavern owner shelled out to buy her share of the building from them. They made a point to keep the old sign and name of the tailor shop, to honor the location's history.

The half-giant that provided security at the front door recognized him with a nod as he entered, which Alnyx returned. The floor was filled with people, sitting at tables, dancing to music provided by a musician with a fiddle and a singer who was mostly on key. The laughter and chatter would mostly drown it out anyway.

"Cousin, good to see you! It's been awhile." Though the elf behind the bar bore the bands of a different family of the Rawanali clans, they were all cousins. And Alnyx was always glad to see when it was her behind the bar. "Your usual ale then?"

"Pine whiskey if you have it, actually."

"A taste of home. Means a good payment ey? Coming up."

Alnyx took time to scan the crowd as he waited, taking one of the empty stools. Elves and giants. Fae and fair. The blend of patrons here always made him feel comfortable. The owner of the place made a point to keep their identity a secret to anyone that didn't need to know, which made it easier for them to serve non-humans with no questioning.

"Here you are." the tankard was placed in front of him, and the other elf leaned on the bar. "I heard from Cinna that you'd made your way up to his neck of the woods not long ago. I was worried you'd lost your sense and good taste."

Alnyx snorted and put a pile of coins on the counter. She took fewer than she should have and tossed them into the collection tin with a clink. Before he answered, Alnyx took a long drink with a content sigh. The sweet smack of pine that accompanied the burn or the whiskey warmed him quickly.

"For a job. Had to take along a mage that was staying there."

"Heard about that partner business. Residentials won't stop bitching about it. You'd think the fool killed someone instead of making another someone. Ridiculous."

Alnyx raised his drink in agreement. The woman tapped her fingers on the wood of the bar in a farewell, going to serve someone else who had walked over. The routine of it settled Alnyx in a way he hadn't realized he had been missing. How had a few days with the horned half-wylder thrown him so far from his axis? They were far from the first pretty face he had come across in this work. The variety and danger of the work drew exactly his type after all. Coupled, most importantly, with the untethered goodbyes.

But the stranger...No. Absinthe. They latched on. Perhaps, he thought, it was the sheer competency that rarely came from Scholars. Their easy way of speaking, and the way they used deflection instead of defensiveness around bigotry. The charming grin. By the ancestor tree, it was charming.

Alnyx knocked back the drink, to numb the thought. He held up a finger when he caught the barwoman's eye.

"A difficult task then." She lingered, taking a few more of the coins in exchange for a refill. "Or is there a different sort of trouble weighing heavy on you, Cousin?"

Alnyx scowled. He didn't have a proper answer. Which he disliked greatly. He wrapped his fingers around the handle of the tankard and stared into it when she didn't leave.

"The sort of difficulty I can call upstairs for you, perhaps?" The question was asked in a lower tone, the woman leaning into his space so they wouldn't be overheard.

It wasn't as if it was a secret, or if it was meant to be, it was poorly kept. The "apartments" above the tavern weren't exactly on a normal sort of rent system. More....Hourly than by the moons. The bar staff had to approve anyone looking to rent for the evening, and kept a protective watch over their tenants. He'd watched more than one bad actor get tossed out by the half-giant. And had....Indulged himself in the past. Too expensive to make a habit of it.

"The flowers are beautiful tonight." she leaned back and continued, picking up a glass to pretend to clean. "All reds and golds."

"Mmmhm." A code he knew. Over the top? Perhaps. "I'm not a floral man. I prefer ferns. Evergreens."

The silver for his drinks was replaced by the last few gold coins from the extra stash that wasn't meant for the caravan spot. She knew he was good for it, but the song and dance is what kept people safe.

"Tried and true, Cousin." she patted his arm before waving one of the people over that cleared empty tankards and filled them again. The second gesture was one he didn't recognize, but was sure it meant to mark his order.

Alnyx left the gold next to his elbow as he took a drink. A stupid way to spend the extra coin. Worse than on the drinks. He could have put it to the side for new leathers. A good oil for his swords. Perhaps even getting the soles of his boots re-

"Good evening, Sir. Is this seat taken?"

The owner of the voice sat before he could answer. Mortal, round in all the placed that creatures like Alnyx were sharp. A plain, dark colored tunic and breaches would have him blending in to the crowd of patrons easily. The gathering of maidenhair leaves tucked behind one eat, pinning blond curls away from his face was the only indication he wasn't one of them.

"It is now."

He laughed, turning to face Alnyx. No one else would hear the little clink as two of the coins at the elf's elbow found their way up the man's sleeve. The fingers lingered, brushing against the elf's arm.

"I've seen you here before, haven't I? I never forget a face. Especially not a handsome one."

Alnyx finally looked at him enough long to meet his eyes. Blue. Lovely, cornflower, blue. Made deeper by the green that framed one side of his face.

"When I'm in town." Alnyx moved the tankard away. And took away the coins that had been for a third round. " 'm usually on the road."

"Well then, how fortunate for me." the mortal kept his hand on Alnyx's elbow. "In fact, I've only just called up for hot water for a bath. I was worried it might go to waste. But for a world-weary traveler? Perfect."

A charmer. More talkative than he might have liked. But beggars could hardly be choosers.

8

Chapter 8

The door to the apartment barely swung closed behind them before Alnyx had the mortal pressed against it, the weight of their bodies what truly allowed the latch to click. The elf's hands dwarfed the man's thin waist as he settled them on either hip. If he tried, he could make his fingertips touch.

"Eight Divines aren't you gorgeous." the charm and talkative nature from the public room quickly became tinged with the right amount of filthy. "This truly must be my lucky night."

Alnyx couldn't help but smirk under the praise. He tightened his grip. Nearly hard enough to bruise. The content, bordering on desperate, groan was confirmation it wouldn't have been unwanted if he had. A shuddering of breath when Alnyx bent his head, lips to the shell of the rounded ear. He took pride in being able to silence the mouthy ones.

"Anything off limits?" Alnyx had the composure to be able to pause and ask. The way he could feel the whole weight of the mortal in his hold said they certainly couldn't.

"Gorgeous, you can do whatever you'd like to me." The whine was followed much more coherently after a beat with "No visible marks. No blood." At least some self preservation.

With that as permission, Alnyx shifted back just slightly. And before the curly haired human could argue, Alnyx pressed their mouths together and swallowed the gasp that it elicited. The mortal tasted like mint. And more than a little like desperation.

"Meant it. About the bath water." The man managed to get his composure back, just barely enough to speak when they parted to breathe properly. "Tub's even big enough for two."

The coin from the contract was good, but not good enough to turn down a free, hot bath. So, Alnyx stepped back and removed his hands from the man's hips so he was no longer pinning him to the wood of the door.

"Ah. Good. I'll just...." The mortal slipped through the gap, pausing to remove his soft-soled shoes. "If you would..."

Alnyx chuckled at the request, but braced one arm against the wall as he removed his boots. The little laugh it got from the other man was comforting, easing any tension that might have built. He wouldn't be the first to reconsider once they really got a look at Alnyx. Wouldn't be the last either, he'd wager the coins he still had left.

"The door over on the left there." the mortal pointed. "Fancy a drink? I don't have the pine stuff you were drinking downstairs. Just regular."

"Sure." As Alnyx walked, he started to strip his shirt off, shaking his head once it was off just before getting to the door. He didn't miss the excited little "fuck" it elicited from the mortal, no matter how quietly he thought he'd said it.

Paid or not, it was always nice to be appreciated. As he stepped into the room with the tub he dipped his fingers into the water, which had been dosed with some sort of soap that gave way to bubbles. The vessel seemed to be spelled with something that helped it keep its heat. Briefly, Alnyx felt bad for interrupting what was clearly meant to be a relaxing night. Only briefly, as he undid the fall of his pants and stepped out of them and into the water.

It was his turn to groan and sigh as he submerged himself. He should have been a little more worried about making a mess, but whatever kept the water warm seemed to keep it from sloshing all over the place as well. Ancestors bless the dependence on mages in the cities, truly.

"Don't you look comfortable." the man entered, with two glasses of a dark colored liquid, and in nothing but a silken robe that was barely tied closed.

The grunt from Alnyx said he was, in fact, quite comfortable. He had closed his eyes almost as soon as the water came up to his chest, but peaked open the other one when he heard the rustling of the silk. Thin, but not in the way one would be if they were going hungry. Pale, unmarked as if he had never seen a day's hard labor. When the glasses were placed on the stool beside the tub, they were joined by the branches that he had still left behind his ear. He shook his head, freeing the curls from their place as the silk slipped fully off his shoulders and pooled onto the miraculously dry floor.

"I hate to ask you to move, looking as you do...But, bunch up a bit so I can get behind you." When Alnyx answered with an arched eyebrow, he continued. "How else am I meant to wash your hair?"

That was...Certainly a new one for him. But, it didn't sound unpleasant. So he shifted forward enough, to allow him to slip behind. He didn't get in the water right away. Instead, the mortal stepped to a vanity, looking through an array of bottles. Bare as the moon that came in from the window, he was truly a sight.

"Is there something I should call you? Besides Sir. You don't seem like the type to prefer master...."

"Alnyx." He was never one for false names. No sense in it.

"Peter." the mortal properly introduced at last. "But you're welcome to call me whatever you like." a wink of those pretty blue eyes as he lifted a few of the small bottles and walked back to the tub.

Peter handed Alnyx one of the glasses so he could set the bottles down, running a hand through the still mostly dry locks. He was gentle as his fingers worked through a few knots they encountered. The pads of them were surprisingly rough and calloused when they traced the lines of the tattoo bands on the shaved parts.

"Most Taskers I've met keep their hair short. Like the military lads. " Peter's voice was a sweet whisper right against the shell of his pointed ear as Alnyx sipped the drink. "Easier to manage and harder to grab in a fight."

"Cultural." was the best explanation that he would get.

"Well. I'll have to take extra good care of it then."

Peter finally stepped into the water, one leg on either side of Alnyx. He started to massage the elf's scalp. A new sensation, and a pleasant one if the fact he closed his eyes again and sighed was any indication. Peter's near constant chatter was replaced with soft humming. Alnyx couldn't place the tune, but he was certain he preferred it over the talking.

"I'm going to get your hair wet now." Peter warned him. "Tilt your head back. Don't want to get it in your eyes."

Cupped hands kept the water mostly to the hair, and far from the elf's eyes. The bottles he'd brought along had some sort of treatment in them. The viscous liquids smelled of citrus and lavender, and tingled the scalp. He was not the sort that....Allowed himself to be pampered. But it was pleasant. Unexpected. And Peter has experience with this sort of treatment, with other elves it seemed when the massage when from hair and scalp to the ears. Just enough pressure to be pleasant. A practiced skill.

He hadn't meant to close his eyes for longer than was needed. But the third glass of Whiskey. Warm water, kind touches. He was only a Man after all. It wasn't a true sleep by any means. Alnyx could still hear every note of the hummed song, and feel every bit of pressure against his scalp. And yet, it was the most rested he had felt in weeks.

"There now." Peter kept his voice soft as he raked the last bit of product on his fingers through, after what could have been hours as far as Alnyx was concerned. "Give yourself a little dunk, and I'll get you a towel." he got out himself, wrapping one around his waist so he could put all the glass, bottles and empty drinking ones, up and out of the way.

Alnyx waited until the breakables weren't in his hands anymore before reaching out and touching him. Well, the poorly tucked in part of the towel at the very least. When it fell away, Peter bent to pick it up. As if he hadn't noticed that it didn't slip on its own.

"Leave it."

From the partially crouched position, on one knee, Alnyx's voice did startle Peter just a little. He looked up at him, and realized quite quickly that the elf's height and hair weren't the only things that were impressive. The mortal's cheeks went pink, his mouth dry when he tried to form some sort of response than "oh fuck yes."

"See something that is more interesting than my hair, Peter?"

"Yes, Alnyx."

"Not Sir?"

"Whatever you'd like."

* * *

Alnyx hadn't expected Peter to crawl forward the way that he did. A short distance, made easier on the knees by the miraculously dry bath mat under them. The mortal sat up and looked at Alnyx, hands folded neatly on his own lap as he was eye level with the elf's navel, decidedly not looking down yet. The blue eyes seemed to take on a darker hue as the lust grew. And Alnyx would be lying if he said it didn't cause him to swallow rather hard.

"This is MUCH more interesting a sight than your hair. And certainly not as....Soft now, is it?" It wasn't thirst that had Peter licking his lips when he looked down.

The fact the mortal was still so confident and chatty was equal parts impressive and frustrating. Impressive that Peter could string together such a witty response, even though he couldn't keep himself from panting or his fingers twitching. Frustrating because even at his best, the elf was at a disadvantage.

Peter settled in to a more comfortable position, the little shimmy causing his own hardening member to bounce and remind him of its existence. But it went ignored as Peter raised his eyes to meet Alnyx's.

"Can't see a soft thing about you from down-"

Alnyx had enough. No matter how clever, the sharp tongue could be used for better things. So before Peter could finish the though, he grabbed a hand full of the thick, blonde, curls which elicited a gasp. The tug on them turned the gasp to a desperate groan, eyes closed as he was directed where Alnyx wanted him to go.

Peter was very used to the scholarly elves who came to meet in Morgranto. Magic users always had extra energy to burn, and their status meant they had deep pockets most of the time to match. Both their men and women were lithe, lean things. Flexible, beautiful, and hairless from the neck down in a way that had felt unsettling the first few times he lay with one. From his wide frame to the thatch of brown hair that the cock in front of him jutted out from, Alnyx was nothing like them. The mortal's fingers twitched, itching to trace the black bands of tattoos that covered the tanned skin in a pattern he was sure meant something. They were faded in some parts by age, marred and scratched in others by scars from his work. And thick, two fingers, almost three in spaces with more real estate like the thighs and abdomen.

Bless the eight divines, they were not the only three-finger-thick thing that Peter saw when he could catch his breath and properly focus again. He reached one hand up from his lap, tracing one of the tattoos upwards from calf to thigh and mirroring it on the other side. Pressing his palm flat just above Alnyx's left hip, the right hand curled around the base of his cock, delighting in the feeling of the coarse curls scratching against it. Thick enough the tips of his fingers brushed barely. Long enough that he could wrap his full other hand around atop the first fist. Oh they did make them bigger in the north.

"Cat got your tongue, Peter?"

Peter's response was wordless. He took the aforementioned tongue and ran it from the edge of his fist under his shaft to the head of Alnyx's cock. He lingered there, lapping up a bead of precum that gathered at the slit. The tightening hand in Peter's hair kept him very still, even as the growl from somewhere above him sent a shiver down his spine. He wrapped his lips around the head, taking great care to make sure his teeth were covered. Already, Peter could tell that his jaw was going to ache in a glorious way come morning.

Alnyx's other hand joined the one already in Peter's hair. The tugging stopped, in favor of him running his fingers through the ringlets only moderately more gently. When Peter leaned his head forward to take more of Alnyx into his mouth with no choked sound, there sharp pulling was renewed. The gag came when Peter made it half way, lips connecting with his fist. He wasn't there long, as Alnyx used his grip to pull the blonde off of his cock. A thin strand of saliva still connected Peter's lips to it as he shifted just enough to meet the elf's eyes.

"Bed." Alnyx grunted as a command, which Peter more than happily scrambled to his feet to obey.

Peter led the way down the small hallway to the only other room with a door in the apartment. Alnyx took the opportunity to watch him walk, eyes trailing along the mortal's back to the narrow hips that seemed to always subconsciously sway in order to draw attention to them. Down the pale, freckle-dusted legs. He didn't go in immediately after him when Peter opened the door and entered. A few breaths to keep his composure, as it wouldn't do to prove the savage reputation right.

What a sight to be greeted with when he did step into the room. It was mostly dark, lit only by an oil lamp on the bedside table. Those long legs spread akimbo as Peter lay on his back, propped up on his elbows so he could look at Alnyx. His thin chest heaved, the pink blush from his cheek extending down it and matching the flush of his cock that was hard against his stomach. Peter was sure to look like he was worth every bit of the coin he was paid, and judging by the pause at the side of the bed, the light grazing of sword-callused fingers against his knee, Alnyx agreed.

"See something that is of more interest than my hair?" Peter stole Alnyx's words which got an amused snort from the elf before the leg he had been touching was pushed to the side.

Alnyx climbed onto the bed, which creaked under the extra weight as he settled between Peter's legs. On his elbows as Peter was, their faces were hardly an inch apart as Alnyx hands settled on either side of his head. The man swooned forward to catch the elf's lips in a kiss, pouting when he caught only air.

"Oil?"

"No need."

"Fuck off, no need." Alnyx scowled. "Oil." Not a question this time.

"Left side top drawer." Peter watched as Alnyx reached over so he didn't have to move. It was charming watching him fumble through the smooth plugs that served as Peter's company on nights he did not work to find the jar. "Really though. It isn't-"

Silenced by a kiss. A tongue probing his mouth since it had been trying to make some silly argument. Peter put his arms around Alnyx's shoulders, trusting the elf atop him would have little problem handling the weight. Alnyx tasted of whiskey, pine, and something deeper and darker that was distinctly Him. Peter was lost in it, craving more as he chased the elf's tongue with his own.

He was so distracted that he hadn't noticed Alnyx had gotten the lid of the jar off with one hand, right next to his head. Peter whined when

Alnyx moved away, falling onto his back as the motion broke the loop of his arms around the elf's shoulders. Turning his head, Peter could watch as Alnyx coated his fingers with the oil. Any complaint he might have made to get him to move faster was gone in a series of hisses and gasps as the slick fingers traced a line down his chest. As one of them slipped past the tight ring of muscle between his legs, the gasps turned to moans, mingled with chanting of "yes please yes".

Alnyx straightened up so he could watch Peter squirm as he worked him loose, using the unoccupied hand to pick the jar back up to bring it closer to their waists. When a second equally slick finger joined the first, Peter raised his arm from where it had fallen at his side. The elf seemed cruelly determined to ignore the mortal's poor, leaking cock, so he would have to handle it himself.

Before Peter could so much as get the tips of his fingers close enough to provide any sort of relief, his wrist was grabbed. Peter whined when Alnyx tossed the arm up above hie head where it hit the mattress again. The other was more purposefully lifted, and Alnyx held them both down in place by the wrists with one of his own. The position meant that Alnyx leaned fully over Peter now. So close that if Peter thrust his hips up, perhaps the friction between their stomachs could be enough.

"Please." he whined, hips jerking upwards, head thrown back as a third finger joined its brothers. "Please. Sir. Alnyx. Whoever you want–I need–Fuck–"

Alnyx had curled one of his fingers, brushing against the bundle of nerves inside Peter that turned pants and desperate whines to a near scream. He made sure to hit it with every movement of his fingers now, taking great, perhaps TOO great, pains to ensure the mortal was prepared.

When Alnyx finally pulled them free, Peter was left painfully empty. The mortal lay the back of his head on the pillow, opening his eyes to glare at Alnyx as a silent order for him to keep on going. But they were glassed over, so there was no real heat to the look. There was a great heat, though, as the blush darkened when Alnyx lifted his hand and licked the fingers that had just been inside of him. The elf shifted back slightly, to pick up the jar again which left Peter's arms unbound.

"Keep them there." He ordered, taking a more substantial pool of oil into the messy hand this time.

To his credit Peter managed both to keep them in place AND give his best attempt at looking devastated. It was as if he had been asked to do something terrible; like kick a puppy or steal sweets from a child. Alnyx chuckled, bending his head and pressing his lips to Peter's clavicle.

"There's a good boy." He straightened again, raising one hand to pat the mortal's cheek

Peter's eyes went soft and his jaw went slack at the praise. He whimpered the same pathetic whine and turned his head. Before Alnyx could take them away, Peter caught the tips of the elf's fingers between his lips. He made sure their eyes met before he parted them wider. There was something dangerous that flashed in Alnyx's eyes before he took the invitation. Three fingers stretched his mouth wide, and Peter was just as careful about his teeth this time as he was before.

Alnyx had no problem pushing his fingers forward, so Peter's lips met the ridge of his first knuckle each and every time. The rapid movement caused gasps and gags with every movement, Peter's eyes rolling to the back of his head. He didn't see the other hand release his wrists, but certainly felt it when those sword-callused fingers wrapped around his throat.

The external pressure on his throat. The fullness of his mouth. The weight of the elf on top of him. I was too much. As Peter's hips jerked upward, the hand around his throat tightened but the fingers were removed from his mouth. As if the elf couldn't bear to muffle Peter's cry when he came.

"Did you just....Fuck you didn't even touch my cock." The words were sputtering, half formed things. Peter wasn't even sure if they were a thought or out loud between pants.

"I am not finished with you yet." And yet, Alnyx sat back.

He was between Peter's legs, both hands running down his chest before pushing Peter's hips flush and spreading them far as they would go. The pause was very intentional as the hands pressed into the meat of his ass before bending him backwards car as he could go. Even as brilliantly exposed as he now had the bard, there was still a pause. The delicious, hedonistic something from before was far from Alnyx's eyes when they met again. Permission. Patience.

"You really are a gentleman." Each word was practically a sentence itself while Peter managed to get them out. "Yes, you beautiful thing you. Keep going."

Peter couldn't give him further permission or encouragement. He was so painfully sensitive when one of the elf's hands finally brushed his cock and it jumped, eagerly trying to rise again. Alnyx didn't try to work him back up to it, descriptively nimble fingers just focusing near the head of it and the ridge under it.

Before Peter could beg or change his mind, there was something more blunt than the fingers at his entrance. The slow ease of Alnyx's hips moving couldn't keep Peter from crying out, throwing his head back. With his legs not being held down in place, he put them over the elf's shoulders instead. The right decision, judging by the purely animal growl it got from Alnyx, and the hand tightening properly around his cock in time with Peter clenching around his own.

The sound of slick skin on skin almost threatened to dwarf the sounds Peter made. And they did when the hand was gloriously around his throat again. Every squeeze Alnyx gave to Peter's throat he matched to one around his cock, timed with each thrust of his hips. The fact he kept it so....Coordinated might have been a marvel to Peter if he could string the thought together.

Suddenly Alnyx pulled so far back only the head of his cock was still in the mortal. Harder than before, enough to slam the headboard against the wall, he snapped forward. Again. And again. He had to remove his hands from Peter, to brace them on the bed and to catch his breath for a moment. The movement meant, however briefly, he slipped fulled out of the human.

"Don't you fucking DARE!" The startled gasp caught Alnyx off caught when the hold the legs had around his waist tightened.

"Who is paying who here, Peter?" Alnyx lined himself back up as he asked the question, directly hitting the bundle of quivering nerves inside Peter.

"I'll charge you double if you come anywhere but inside me. Now fuck me, you bastard."

And how could he say no to such a mutually beneficial request? Every thrust now followed the same line that hit Peter's prostate. Keening, desperate crying mingled with every panting breath from the both of them.

When the man's cum painted both of their chests, Alnyx gave one last thrust and a gasp. Peter swallowed the sound, leaning up to kiss the elf, hands in his hair as he kept him close as they both rode out Alnyx's orgasm. Alnyx only just managed to keep from falling on him with his whole body weight, forehead against Peter's shoulder as he lowered himself onto his elbows, their breath mingling as they stayed so close.

"I don't suppose you can call for another bath?" felt his eyes drifting closed as Peter played with his hair.

"If you think I'm moving anywhere before morning, you're mad."

Alnyx shifted, so he was laying beside Peter now, limbs all but limp as the exhaustion crept into him.

"You're going to be mad about it in the morning."

"That's a problem for morning Peter." Before the elf could even suggest leaving, Peter put his arms around him. "Morning Alnyx as well. Tomorrow us. Sleep now."

9

Chapter 9

Alnyx was still up with the sun, which was a surprise to him after the previous night's activities. With Peter's limbs tangled around him as they were, he had to take great care not to wake the mortal as he freed himself. Alnyx shoved the pillow into the void of the human's arms, pausing to make sure his eyes didn't open. Satisfied Peter's sleep was undisturbed, he walked to the bathroom.

Before pulling his clothes back on, making sure they were his and not the smaller man's, he took a moment to assess himself in the mirror. His hair was clean, but a mess he would have to sort out when he had access to his things. And a rag and cold water from the wash basin would have to do to clean up any...Remaining evidence from the night before.

Once his boots were on, he was out the door they had been so neatly left next to. He searched his pockets for the strap of leather he kept in them to keep his hair out of face, since it would be the best he could do.

The tavern was empty while the sun was up, and so the cleaning girls were the only ones in the large room. They whispered among themselves as he came down the stairs, pausing to use a mirror by the bar. The guard at the door grunted when he made his way over, and Alnyx gave a nod in response.

"I wasn't able to lock the door. If someone could do so for him?"

It shouldn't have been a kindness. Should have just been common courtesy. Judging by the confusion it got from the half giant (a different one from the night before, only noticeable by a scar above one brow), it was not though. But the guard nodded and Alnyx set out onto the street.

The walk back to the Bed-share was a good one. His muscles were pleasantly sore and the stretch it provided helped him to loosen up some. He picked up a loaf of bread, and some dried sausage from one of the early morning vendors. In this distract it cost more, but certainly tasted better than the dried fish and day old rolls that he'd find closer.

"Oh you must be the wolf's human then." The young man behind the desk beamed when Alnyx gave his name and bed number to him. "Or…Elf rather. The night worker said he'd been a darling. Tucked himself in and everything."

Alnyx couldn't help but smile. The lycine knew how to get what he wanted as easily as any two-legged beast did. Even if what he usually wanted was food he shouldn't eat.

"Good. Thank you." he nodded to confirm he was before going up to the bed-share room.

Seeing his fury companion curled up and dreaming, he almost felt bad for nudging him awake. Almost. Fish peaked an eye open and yawned, giving a sleepy whimper before covering his snout with one paw.

"Your tricks don't work on me, don't try to play cute." Alnyx picked up his bag from where it had been stashed under the bed. "Up. We have a lot of ground to cover before it gets dark." No movement on top of the bed. "We're off to The Grove, remember?"

The other eye opened, and Fish stretched out, rising onto his paws. He let out another mighty yawn before shaking the blanket off. The beast jumped from the bed to the floor, with a few wags of his tail.

"Thought that might do it. We'll get you something fresh from the butcher and head out. I want to make it to the lake by nightfall."

At the mention of the butcher, the snow-white beast was already half way to the door without looking back. A fond chuckle and an adjustment of his bag's straps, and Alnyx was on the way behind him.

***

Even though it was stationary, unlike the nomad bands that his Father and Mother led, every trip to The Ancestral Grove of his clan seemed to take longer than the last. Even if it started in the same place most times. Every hour further from the salty spray of Port Morgranto's air, he could feel the giant pine trees call to him.

The snow was nothing more than a troublesome flurry in the few days it took to move along the well-trod path to the last Northern City of Humanity. The bed in the Inn was only marginally softer than the ground, but it was at least dry. And the water was heated by metal pipes and magics like further south. The little town had come up quite a bit since his last stay there seven, maybe nine, years ago. More surprising than the warm water, though, was the newly sanctioned Tasker Guild office.

There were more beasts than people up here, and even fewer of them would have had the coin needed to make a proper request. When Alnyx stopped in before he meant to be on his way in the morning, it was more out of curiosity and perhaps to have a good story for Marigold in case a trinket or a gift wasn't possible. But seeing the desperation on the man's face behind his desk, the elf could not help himself. The work that was local was mostly clearing out beast nests, making the surrounding area little more...Hospitable for the locals and the few traders that made their way though. The payments were part in coin, but mostly in a trade of goods or services.

The beautifully preserved leather bracers, perfect for an offering to the Elders he decided, were too enticing to pass up. And considering it was a rare enough thing to have a warrior capable this far up, there was no need to profit share. Thank the Ancestors for what Marigold had called "approved exceptions".

Two and a half days later than he had originally planned on, with furs, leathers, and even a little more coin, Alnyx and Fish made their way to the treeline of his clan's Grove. He took pause, placing a bare palm against the bark. The rough scratches from it were more pleasure than pain, a familiar abrasion. A few decades of climbing through the branches and falling out of them came to mind. The roots never forgot their saplings.

By the time he opened his eyes again, Fish was already ahead, a blur of white as the lycine moved through the trunks and boughs. The joyous howling of the beast made any subtle entrance impossible. But Alnyx could not help but chuckle fondly as he followed after. Even though Fish was the most magical thing about him, branches and boulders seemed to shift out of the way to give him a bath to safely walk. More than one bent towards him instead, tangling in stray strands of his hair, like the hands of a mother fussing over their messy child come in from playing outside.

"Well well. Look what the Dryads dragged in. You certainly know how to make an entrance, Little Leaf. Fish could wake a sleeping giant with all that racket."

Not a scout from his people, but just as welcome a sight as one may have been. He knew those hoof-beats nearly as well as he knew his own footsteps as he turned to face the female voice. The body of a dappled gray horse gave way to the torso of a woman from the waist up. Her laugh shook the very trunk of the tree that she stepped out from behind of to properly greet him. There were few people that ever made Alnyx feel small, though he supposed that the Centaur wasn't... Well, people exactly.

"Iphinica." he smiled and stood before her. "You try to tell Fish to be calm or behave himself. He hardly knows the meaning of either one."

"That's why he has always been my favorite." She bent, their foreheads pressing together as a sort of embrace. "Walk with me. I will take you to Your Grove." There was a familiar mischief in those violet eyes.

"Of course." he took a half step bask so she could lead the way.

As if he needed a guide in these woods.

"It has been far too many moons since you have been back. Has something happened?" She stepped over a large, exposed, root with more ease on four legs than Alnyx could do with two. "You smell of people and of the ocean."

"Nothing out of the ordinary." A small lie. The encounter with the Scholar has been anything but ordinary after all. "I was in the Port town that I have told you about in the past. And the Human town just a half day journey from here before then."

"I see...Nothing out of the ordinary, and yet you have been called to The Grove for the first time in nearly as many years as you have fingers, close to the snow you may have to wait to thaw before returning to your Wandering." Iphinica arched an eyebrow. "You do not seem wounded. Nor does Fish."

"Can't I just come home like any traveler without having to have a reason?"

"You are not just any traveler, Little Leaf." She laughed and shook her head, causing her hair to shift just slightly from the way it lay covering her otherwise bare chest. "The Forest is always glad for the return of her saplings. But you know that your nosy clan-mates will not be so easily put off as I may be from answers."

Alnyx was all too aware of that fact. The youngest among them were always the easiest to redirect with a stories of cities and places they had never heard of outside of a book or a passing nomad. His direct blood could be contented with knowing he was in one piece and well kept. It was the Elders and the Treespeakers themselves that were the problems. The specific probing about the Winding Trails. The demands to be party to new definitions and visions since he saw the world outside of the trees…He already planned on leaving if the questions went beyond fifteen in the first meeting.

"With luck, the need to prepare of the change in seasons will be enough to keep them preoccupied."

Iphinica's laugh said she didn't believe it either. She waited for him to navigate past another particularly curious bramble bush that had gotten its hooks into his pant leg.

"I met someone." he relented when he managed to get the pointy bit out of the fabric without tearing anything or harming the bush. But wasn't able to get any other words out before he was interrupted.

"Alnyx!" The centaur gasped before he could elaborate. "Someone? But…" The beaming grin faltered as she glanced around. "I see only you and Fish here."

"Not that sort of someone." Alnyx rolled his eyes. "On a job. They were part Wylder, and speaking with them about it made me homesick."

"Part Wylder? By that messy hovel by the ocean? Those sort do not go that far." Iphinica wrinkled her nose as she considered it. "At least not any who belong to reputable covens. You are sure?"

"It is what they claimed, and they gave me no reason not to believe them." Alnyx shrugged in return, wiping dirt from his hands off onto his pants. "We only spoke briefly about it, and it felt wrong to pry."

Alnyx recounted the details of the conversation, as much as what might matter to the horse woman. A cult of the Green, from a grassland that had to be nearer the Highblood Towers and the mages than here. A father that hadn't been a mortal man, or stayed around for long enough to explain themselves. When Iphinica asked how he could tell, he explained the horns, but was sure he did them no justice. The notion some grazer-horned Wylder was roaming around had her wracking her brain for which of the Covens would allow for that and kept her from asking questions Alnyx didn't have answers to.

Eventually Fish did re-join them, likely able to tell they were growing closer to the settlement. Already the white fur was a dirty brown-gray as the beast had been happily rolling in Ancestors know what while they were apart. But the happy way the lycine's tongue lolled as he jumped from fallen log, to rock, to tree stump made him hard to stay annoyed with. Even Iphinica kept from groaning when he licked her hand.

He could smell The Grove before there was any sight of it, on the ground or in the massive, thickening canopy above them. The sweet scent of flower and herb gardens, cultivated longer than the spans of mortal lives, cut with the char from the smoke houses that helped preserve kills from hunts when game was more scarce. There was the whisper of chattering families and traders as they neared the Center on the Floor. So many voices in his native tongue, Alnyx found a place inside his chest he hadn't realized had grown cold grow warmer.

10

Chapter 10

"Well now. Silver said Iphinica had picked up a wanderer. But this is a surprise."

The voice preceded the dull thud of its owner jumping from the low hanging branch they had been perched on and onto the ground. A female elf, dressed in the brown and red leathers of a scout. Her shaved head bore tattoos in clear shapes of vines and leaves, the white ink of them a sharp contrast to dark skin made deeper from a life lived outside. She grinned as her eyes met Alnyx's, who smiled in return.

"Cousin. Good to see you as well. It is not a bad time for my visit, I hope?"

"The Grove always welcomes her saplings home." She answered as if by wrote, the two clasping forearms in greeting. "Are you planning to winter with us as well? The Wyrd Warden believes we are not far from the snows coming."

"No, not so long. A fortnight at the longest." Several months with his extended family was nearly enough to cause his flight or fight instincts to kick in. "I will help with whatever preparations are still needed. I wouldn't want to burden your mother for giving me a roof while I am here."

"And will we have to pay for the privilege of your assistance as they do in the cities, Child of the Wind?"

"Elder Saseshan." Iphinica was the first to turn around. "I was just escorting Alnyx here. I'll be going now."

The look she gave Alnyx was apologetic, but only just. He couldn't blame her: the filly was never one for unscheduled politicking or pleasantness. And the presence of an Elder almost always meant both. Iphinica embraced Alnyx briefly before turning and going back the way they had walked up. He waited until her form disappeared behind a tree to turn back around.

"Of course not, Elder." he only briefly met the milky-blue eyes, which saw nothing but still pierced into him. "We provide for one another. I bring gifts."

The extra furs from clearing out a few bears that went to close to the mortal settlement were easier to present than the bracers still tucked safely under them. Alnyx did not preset them to the Elder, but to the guard that had been standing silently to one side, who took them without having to be told to.

"And what is it you expect us to provide to you? After you bring no word for-"

"Elder." His cousin scolded as gently as they could manage. "He has only just arrived again. Let us get a meal in him a night's rest before we pry into the state of the world."

The ancient, white-haired, glass-eyed elf scoffed, but waved their hand in a clear dismissal. Alnyx and the scout didn't need to be told twice, both bowing at a ninety degree angle with their palm flat against their breast bone as was proper before scurrying away. Towards the winding staircase that the scout had ignored on their way down.

"You're more than welcome to stay in my home." the offer was a statement, not a question. "Dhocut left us to join the New Growth about six moons ago. He wedded a girl from there, so the bed has been empty."

"Married?" Alnyx frowned, a brief pang of guilt. "I didn't know."

"You are harder to get a hold of than your parents, Cousin." she pointed out, shaking her head. "It was a union of convenience, not adoration. They needed a Hunter, and he needed a wife. According to his mother at any rate."

"Some things never change." There was a sorrow that tinged the shared little laugh. "Thank you. Fish and I will be glad to stay with you. And we will try to not cause too much trouble."

The home was nestled high in the branches, next to if not connected to those of other members of the family. All the older homes of the First families were built in the same way: communal, with some limited private spaces. Usually just for adults: children belonged to the Roots until they were of age. Given the time of day, the rooms were all nearly empty since all the able bodied Rawanali were out working or doing chores.

"On the left up there. The second door." The scout pointed and then patted him on the shoulder. "Rest. We will wake you for the evening meal. If I'm not back on patrol soon they'll send someone to find me."

Alnyx was happy to follow the direction. His bag hit the ground just inside the door after he closed it, sword belt and boots both following with dull thuds. The room itself was sparse since its inhabitant left: little more than a bed, desk, and wash basin. But the blankets were woven by the hands of the family matriarch. The fur rug was a trophy of a hunt decades old. Even the desk and dresser were carved by hand from the very wood of the trees they were in.

A bone-deep weariness settled as he fell onto the bed, nose pressed to the pillows as he inhaled soap, sap, and something floral. He didn't even kick Fish back out of the bed when he felt the dirty beast's warmth against his back and side.

He couldn't recall the last time he fell asleep so quickly.

* * *

Alnyx did manage to wake himself up before he had to be woken, but he didn't leave the bed right away, enjoying just how soft the pillow was, and how comforting the quilted blanket. He could hear the clattering and laughter from what he assumed was the kitchen not far from the room that he had been given. The bed-shares he usually stayed in meant he was accustomed to sleeping with noise around, but this wasn't noise. This was the sound of a community, of a family. He couldn't help but smile as well when he heard peals of laughter and the pattering of young feet across the wood. He sat himself up, looking around the room for Fish, not surprised when he found him absent of the room. There were far too many people who could beg for food scraps from out there. Or scratches behind the ear. He couldn't fault him looking for more pleasant company than they usually were afforded.

"Ah good, you're up." The cousin who had led him here stuck h er head in the door frame. "Supper should be ready shortly if you're up for dealing with others. Fresh off the hunt. I changed the water in the wash basin for you too. Come down when you're ready."

He yawned in response which got him a chuckle before she walked back down the hall. He considered for a moment just staying in the room, sneaking out for food later from the cold box when they had all gone to bed. But, they were giving him a place to stay and they didn't have to. It was the least that he could do.

Alnyx was sure they wouldn't mind a bit of dust from the road hanging on to his clothes, so he didn't bother changing into the fresh things he had brought along yet. He did take the time to go to the basin and get some of the worst of the dirt from his face. He swished a cupped palm full of the water into his mouth before it was too grimy to rinse the sleep from it, and took a few moments glancing at himself in the polished silver of the mirror to make himself presentable. Or at least tame his hair from where it was sticking up in places thanks to the pillow.

"There he is. Worried we'd have to call for a healer if you stayed in that bed much longer."

"Could hear you snoring from up the road! How you haven't been ransacked by bandits before is beyond me. Sleeping like the dead makes for the dead."

There were too many names for him to keep straight; he'd given up on trying two or three prolonged visits ago. At least, this was the case for the cousins that were close enough to his age to be his contemporaries. They moved houses, married and separated, widowed and rejoined, all too quickly for him to keep proper track. Besides, he was hardly more than a name and a story from the elders to most of them.

"It isn't often I have the comfort of a proper bed." He took the empty chair that had been left for him at the table, running his fingers through Fish's dense fur when he plopped down at his side. "Had to take advantage, since I'll be put to work come dawn."

"Nonsense, you're our guest. We can spare you a few hours after the sun rises." The aunt that was the head of the house here was at his side, loading up his plate with vegetables from the garden and elk meat still steaming it was so fresh from the fire. "It is good to see you, Wanderer. Eat first. Then you can tell us of your journey from the south."

Ancestors bless the woman for her understanding. And for her words making sure all the others also turned their attention from him to their plates, at least for the moment. As he sank his teeth into the tender flesh, he couldn't keep himself from letting out the content sigh. His adventures brought him to far flung places, with exotic fare and folk. But there were few things as perfect as a simply dressed elk and greens that were still wet from the dirt rinsed from them.

Once he cleared his plate, and hie belly quieted its grumblings, he was more than willing to give them the story of the hunt in the Kingswood. It was more interesting than clearing out troublesome beasts from the meager farmlands the humans had. He kept to the most important details; the way it fought, and how it had been slain. They didn't need to know the acid veins of the horned Scholar. Or the way he had fussed over the wounds that had left only minimal scars. It would only bring more questions, and this was more than he had spoken at one time in moons as it was.

"A corruption of the ley lines, and fracturing?" One of the uncles frowned, leaning back his chair onto two legs and twisting his fingers in his goatee. "So far from a true source. The last nomad messenger, half a cycle ago, brought rumors of such from further west. We have seen no such thing here."

Alnyx grunted, pausing to take a sip of the warm tea, sweetened with honey that had been given to him. "I hadn't planned to bring it to the Elders. Far enough away, I assumed they would be....Uninterested."

Half the old bastards care for nothing further than their arm could reach. He took another, longer, sip to keep himself from saying as much.

"If it is related to the rumors brought before them, they may need to hear it. They'll be expecting you tomorrow. It may not hurt to mention it."

"Expecting me?" Alnyx had hoped to have more time before sitting before the council of elders. At least more than a day.

"Elder Saseshan wasn't quiet about seeing you and the centaur when you made your way in." One of the cousins partially covered their mouth when they chewed, to feign politeness. "The whole of the Grove likely knows by now. Working or not, someone will be here at sunrise looking for you I'll bet."

Alnyx wrinkled his nose, and the warm cup couldn't hide that or the sigh he couldn't keep back. He could respect the Elders, sure. Had been trained to do so even when he was part of the nomad pack with his mother and father. It did not equal a desire to bow his head blindly. He wouldn't be able to turn away a summons from them without consequences, even if he was was tired. They growled and grit their teeth about his being out in the world as it was, even if it was by the word of–

"I will deal with that, no need to worry Sapling." his aunt clapped her thin hand on his shoulder and gave it a reassuring squeeze. "You are my sister's son, and so you are mine. And I can only imagine how annoyed with me she would be if I let them call upon you while you still have the scent of the Road on your skin."

"Thank you." Alnyx meant it sincerely. "You said there was a messenger half a cycle ago. Have you….Seen my mother or father recently? I had thought maybe with the season shift…."

"You know how they are, Sapling." She shook her head. "The Windriders never stick around long enough to get more than a rod or two in before they're gone again."

"How long ago do you think was the last time? That you heard from them directly."

"Eight, maybe nine moons ago." she gave his shoulder another squeeze. "We would know if there was something worth knowing. And would send word to you. You are always welcome here even without them."

"Thank you." a little less sincere, but he smiled for her sake and finished the mug of warm tea.

It was impossible to escape an evening of drinks on the balconies that were shared between the neighboring families among the boughs of the great trees. They were cordial, most of them curious more than anything. And while it was wonderful to watch Fish run and play with other Watchers, weaving between legs and under tables. he could feel his patience for civility waning.

He managed to politely excuse himself from the matriarch of one of the families, who had been trying to insist it was her duty to help him find a match at the Circle where the priestesses saw who should belong to whom, back against the door as he slipped into his family's home once more. One of the cousins who had stayed behind to make sure the young ones were properly tucked into their beds caught him and couldn't help but laugh.

"Let me guess. Once of the mothers trying to get you to meet and marry her progeny?"

"That obvious?"

"I know the look of someone who has had the displeasure of being cornered by Hethi. She's been trying to get her youngest tied off to anything with a pulse because she can't stand having to keep minding them." He shook his head, motioning for Alnyx to enter properly. "If she asks after you, I"ll tell her you're tired from your journey. Permitting you join us for a hunt if you can get out of that meeting tomorrow morning."

"Gladly. Thank you cousin."

Perhaps Alnyx should have felt a little bit of shame, that all it took was one over-eager matriarch to send him running with his tail between his legs quicker than any contract he'd taken in months. But when he went back to the bedroom, seeing a low burning fire keeping it warm and a rough-spun jerkin clearly for sleeping left for him, he couldn't feel anything but a contentment tucked tightly behind his breastbone. If pushy parents and judgmental Elders were the price to pay for respite, he would suffer happily.

11

Chapter 11

They were blessed with a beautiful morning for a hunt. Six of them went out with Alnyx in the mix, the Watchers among their party scouting ahead of them. Two little parties of three, tasked with bringing back the best kill that they could before the midday meals. Naturally it became a competition quite quickly, but by no means a serious one. The laughter across the boughs and playful sabotage threatened to send them all home empty handed more than once.

As it was, they carried back with them a decent sized boar and a few larger fowl whose feathers would be welcomed by the Fletcher more than their flesh. One of the group has gotten caught in an "innocently placed" snare and so limped form a tender ankle, but it was more a wound of pride than a true injury. They handed off their spoils to those who would butcher and preserve the meats and skins, going to one of the group's homes to enjoy a drink in victory. The wine was overly sweet on Alnyx's tongue, but he sipped it contentedly. He was sure even with his aunt's promise to keep the Elders from bothering him for at least a day, there would be word awaiting him from them when he returned.

Once the mug was empty, he said his farewells, with a promise to do this again before he was back out on his own. The clapped hands on his shoulders made it feel more like he was going off to war than back up to a resting place. He was in no rush, and did not even begrudge Fish for every time the lycine stopped to chase after a pleasing scent. Alnyx nodded pleasantly when acknowledged, doing his best to mostly stay out of the way and out of sight as he and Fish made their way back up the ramp to the house.

His aunt was in the main room of the house, a mountain of correspondence beside her that she was slowly picking her way through. Notes about him certainly, but also just things that were all in a day's work of running an ancient family. She looked over at him as he entered, setting the envelope in her hand to the side and patting the spot next to her on the padded bench. Fish took it before Alnyx could which made the both of them chuckle a little.

"Naughty thing." And yet she still gave the beast a little scratch behind his ears. "The hunt was a good one then? You look pleased."

"It was, thank you." he nodded in response. "Has there been...Word from the Elders?"

"Oh nearly as soon as you were out the door." she shook her head. "As expected. I told them that you were not going to flee and they could wait until tomorrow. They'll be expecting you after the morning meal. I will escort you there myself."

A few more hours of respite then. He could have kissed the woman if she hadn't already picked up the envelope she had put down. And her other hand remained on the lycine who was already more than half asleep with his giant head on her thigh. It was a dismissal at least for now, which Alnyx didn't mind taking.

On the walk back to the room, he contemplated what he would need to bring with to the summons. He had made sure to pack away the "nicest" of this clothing, really just the brown and green leathers that bore the crest of his father's nomadic clan, which he only wore when he was here. Or needed to remind himself he was the son of a leader and his life mattered for more than just a bounty. At least to a few people.

And then there was the matter of a suitable offering, the furs that he'd collected as payment. Originally he was going to give them the gloves, but they hardly deserved them. They were fine things, Elder Saseshan's hands undeserving of them. Perhaps he would give them to his aunt instead. He nodded as he decided this at the threshold to the room.

Alnyx frowned when he saw that his bag had been moved to the chair from where he had placed it, opened and things moved. He looked to the desk though, relaxing a little when there was a note of some kind, atop a neatly folded pile of fabric. A proper cloak, pants and a jerkin that hadn't been stitched and re-stitched a dozen or more times, or fallen out of the bag and into mud and slop.

Considering you have to travel rather light in your work, I assumed correctly you didn't have much that was proper for a meeting with the Elders. I took your spares and family leathers to patch and clean today, but I don't know if they'll be ready before you need them. You can thank me by not being too hard on my borrowed clothing.

It was signed by one of the cousins he guessed had to be close enough to his size to make the offer. Alnyx had packed the clothes near the top of the bag, so it wasn't like they would have had to dig through and see anything private. How often he forgot that privacy and personal belongings were not truly a thing among the people of the Grove. The main doors didn't have locks, let alone the individual bedrooms. Alnyx shook off the discomfort that settled around his shoulders, closing the door so he could get at least some privacy since Fish was already content to be his Aunt's lap dog for now.

He shucked off the clothes that trailed dirt on them from the hunt, piling them in the corner of the room with every intention to ask where the laundry was nowadays, so he could clean them himself to be less of a burden on his cousins. He picked up the sleeping clothes from the night before, settling just on the slightly too long shirt before laying on the bed with a sigh. The comforting fur was warm and only tickled his thighs a little bit.

It was....Something else to have time to decompress, and a space to do so. He closed his eyes, taking in the still, comforting silence of the house. It was empty only of bodies, but their energy was very much still there. The night before he had bristled against it, being out and among all of them. It wasn't that he was unused to the attention, but it was rarely so....Positive. Easier to turn away when people were cold or cruel. As if to perfectly argue all the stereotypes, the Rawanali were far from when it came to one another. Mostly at least. He managed to avoid lingering too long on thoughts of Elder Saseshan and those who followed him like hunting hounds.

Instead he briefly thought back to the matriarch who was so set on marrying him off to her child. To be free of them, his cousin had said. And wasn't that a particularly grim way to think of bonding families: freedom from having to care for someone you were tired of, especially with their long lives.

The idea of being tied to someone though. That he did occasionally think about, and perhaps more than normal during the trip up to the Grove. Not that he would have admitted it unless pressed to do so. With something sharp at the very minimum. Bodily harm always made things easier.

He ran his fingers briefly over his own ribs, closing his eyes to recall the way the bruises had looked after the fight with the gelatinous ley beast. The blooms of deep purple, an almost bloody crimson from the pressure and compression. The pain from each breath when his lungs inflated against his battered ribs, that was nothing new. And they were nothing in comparison to the pressure of long, charcoal fingers pressing against the tender flesh.

Absinthe's fingers were warm on their own, but had been made warmer from the spell weaving they had done. The smell of sulfur cut through even the odor of the salve when they had been so close. And an undercurrent of something herbal, even with the dead earth that had been there. He wondered if it was naturally, or something that he word. With the horned scholar's fondness of fine things, it seemed only natural it would extend to scent as well.

He let out a phantom of a wince as he pressed too hard. Far harder than Absinthe had done. He had watched the long, thin fingers as they worked their way through spidery spells, and the care and seriousness they took. It seemed at odds with the way they had hacked apart the beast's core for parts. He hadn't said it then, but Absinthe found it oddly attractive; the way the scholar hadn't flinched as they dragged the blade through the fleshy core.

* * *

It made him ponder what else the ferocious, elegant fingers could do. The nails were sharp, not quite bestial claws, but perhaps not too far from them. Would they flay skin if the horned scholar put any sort of pressure on the pads of the fingers? Alnyx only half realized he was trailing his hand along the path he imagined them moving. From the formerly battered ribs to hip. They would be direct. Calculating, not easily distracted. It seemed their natural state, after all.

With his eyes closed, it was easy for Alnyx to pretend the fingers that curled around his slowly hardening cock weren't his own. The callouses were from prepping ingredients and pulling literal flames from the weave. The motions of the wrist long, slow and languid. They were the sort that took their time with luxurious, needless things. Like tea and brandy in the mornings. A slow stretching routine to stay limber that Alnyx had watched from the corner of his eye.

He could recall each bend and movement now. The way their spine contorted and bent, and then lengthened slowly. Painfully, he thought.

But each sigh, almost moan, from their lips said maybe there was something to all that. His hand sped, fingers tightening their grip as Alnyx wondered for a moment just how far back their legs could bend. Would their ankles make it over their shoulders? And could they keep them there.

Acid green eyes, blown wide with pleasure, a hiss of his name in a puff of breath from their lips as his body jerked upwards and spent over a hand that was far from slender and lithe.

Alnyx swore to himself, wiping the spend onto the sheet, unable to be bothered to get up and properly clean it. A small miracle that it had missed the fur, but he'd gladly take it. Tossing the sheets in with whatever else might need to go to the laundry was easier than cleaning cum out fur. Something he knew all too well.

Chapter 12

"Well now, don't you clean up nicely." His aunt cupped his fave in her hands, smiling briefly and stepping up onto her toes to press their foreheads together when they met in the morning. After the morning meal, to give him time to prepare and something in his stomach. "You look so much like him."

Him. Her brother in marriage, Alnyx's father. The Nomadic Leader who taught him to crave Movement and the Journey with his every breath. She didn't have to say more than the reverent "him" for it to be clear who she meant. He closed his eyes, taking in the words as the warm compliment they were meant to be.

"Right then. We shouldn't keep them much longer. They'll already no doubt be annoyed with the both of them. Best not give them more reason to fuss.

Alnyx sighed and stepped away first, so he could give one last look over the furs he meant to bring as tribute to the Elders directly. Because apparently wisdom demanded tribute separate from its people. He swallowed the thought and gestured to for his aunt to lead. He kept half a step behind her, to make sure she was in the lead on the trip out of respect for her. And perhaps so he could, admittedly petulantly, scuff his boots and drag his heels.

The Elders spent their days, when they weren't out harassing new arrivals, in the Heart of The Grove. The tallest, most ancient of the towering trees. There, they served as the "political" voice of the Clans, one or two representatives of multiple families and settlements, when it came to interactions with the outside world and other races. For the Grove directly they also would decide on distribution of goods and what and where to plant or hunt and forage. The sort of things that the Elders of any proper, stationary, settlement would have to do.

Each of the original families were represented, and more recently some of the ones who had proven their heartiness after the last brutal winters. Sometimes, a Wandering brother or sister would make their way back and stay at the table for a time. And then of course there were the Leyreaders and Priestesses of the Hunt and Sky.

Stepping inside the hollowed out pine, Alnyx always felt like he was somewhere he shouldn't be allowed to be. Like sneaking in to his parents bedrooms, or the back room of a shop that was owned by someone particularly impatient with the public. The main entrance hall was silent and sterile in a way he imagined the libraries of the Alabaster Square had to be. One of the younger folks, a messenger who tended to the needs of the Elders of the Table, met the two of them and led them up to the lounge where they were expected. Not be the entire council, mind. No, there were far too many important things for them to be doing. Alnyx couldn't be blamed if he didn't mentally beg the ancestors that Saseshan wouldn't be among those that could make time for him.

Fate was rarely so kind to him in that way, so why should it start to change now? At least it was not only the white-haired, sour-faced elder that was settled among the comfortable looking lounges with the remnants of a late breakfast on the table in the center of them. There were two others with him, a local family that he was sure he should recall the name of and the rare kindness of fate after all: a visiting nomadic

Elder, from the tribe of his parents judging by her adornment of feathers all across the her shoulders and deep makeup.

"Windcaller Pitridae."

"Child of the Khan." the woman cooed with affection and stood, holding her hands out in a clear means to embrace him. "I was worried Saseshan had been mistaken when he said that he saw you were here."

His aunt beside him tapped his arm, motioning to take the furs which he handed over so he could step to Pitridae. The scent of fire and fresh hair clung to each ringlet of her long hair. She felt more of home than even the comfortable beds had. She tipped her head, shorter in stature but larger in spirit, and their foreheads touched.

"Had I known you were with us, I would have skipped the hunt yesterday. Apologies for keeping you waiting." he said it loud enough for the other two elders to hear, and Piitridae's laugh made him grin.

"I would never ask a warrior to forsake a hunt just to entertain us." she released him and stepped back. "And you bring your mother's sister to join us as well. Fine payment for your tardiness."

The two women embraced similarly with another hand off of the furs before all were again seated. Tea was poured fresh by the attendant, steaming as Alnyx cupped the mug in his hands.

"I bring fine pelts. Rewards from a hunt on my way here. The human settlement, a day's travel from the edge of the Grove, has grown more sturdy since I was last here." he gestured to the pile, which the attendant picked up to take away for now. "They have set up a post for the people I work with in the larger cities. It would be good for you to know them."

Saeshan's snort of a scoff said exactly what he thought of that idea. But truly, close as they were to the Grove, people were going to be hurt if they didn't approach things carefully.

"I am sure the humans will stick to their boundaries. They have so far." the other elder, another man who seemed too young in the face for the title until you saw the wrinkles around his eyes, spoke to reassure that he was heard. We have watched closely. But it may not hurt to send a party to speak with them."

"A peaceful party." The windcaller nodded. "It would be less helpful to send armed hunters to reaffirm what has been, I assume, an agreeable coexistence."

The fact she got no argument was a good enough indication that she was right. There was a brief moment of calm, chatting about the settlement. Alnyx was even able to explain what it exactly WAS that the Tasker guild did, and how he came about the pelts. It did not make complete sense to them, but they saw no harm or trouble in it at least.

"I am sure, however," Saseshan said once he wrapped up his explanation. "That you did not come so far north to tell us things we already know of the human problem, or to spin some tale of culling problematic beasts."

"Am I no longer allowed to visit my family?" Alnyx tried to keep his temper under control. The gentle hand from his aunt on his arm helped. He swallowed a drink of tea before speaking again. "I ask only because if the visions of the Priestesses have changed, I was not made aware."

"They have not changed. But it is a strange time of year to come for a joyous reunion." The too young elder spoke again. "An...interesting omen, to churn the soil in the time it is meant to rest and rot."

One of the Leyweavers, or a father from their lines at the very least, then. It would be impossible to get away from seeing the Priestesses soon, with how closely they always seemed to work together.

"A brief rest among a resting home." His aunt pointed out. "Perhaps more-so a reminder that though there are some of us who move with the wind and where it takes us, they are still Of Us."

His mother's family and their calming tongue had always been a gift, his father said it regularly. The Windcaller noted it as well judging by her soft smile and approving nod. Saseshan was not so easy to sway, nor did Alnyx think that he would have been.

So instead, he re-told the story of the hunt in the woods yet again. Tracking the beast, and the way it had pulled all the life from the land around it seemed more important to include this time. And perhaps he was a little more…Generous, more specific when he spoke of Absinthe and the work they did. Their knowledge of the leyline, and the words they had for the fracture and feathering. The look his aunt gave him said the change did not go unnoticed.

"This is still far enough away from our lands, but it would seem not so isolated as we thought it to be." the youthful man rubbed a hand across his close-cropped beard. "But an ill omen indeed. If the corruption would spread northward, it would become our concern."

"We will need to seek guidance from the Ancestors." Even the Windcaller's tone was serious now as she looked at Alnyx again. "You were good to bring this to use, Little Breeze."

"Two of the scouting parties will adjust their routes to trace the lines that work their our Wood. Send word to the centaurs and giants that we will seek to meet." Saseshan gave this command to the attendant that Alnyx had almost forgotten was still present.

Given there was now work to be done, Alnyx took it as a wordless dismissal. A correct thing to do, judging by the fact his aunt stood only a few seconds before he did. The Windcaller did as well, so he couldn't get away quite so quickly. They both smiled as they again embraced, foreheads touching and Sharing Breath. She felt like freedom.

The two left quietly, to the eerie silence of the center of the Great Tree, broken by the ever-present noise of the shared center of the Grove's settlement. Tension Alnyx hadn't truly realized he'd been holding until his shoulders dropped left his body with a heavy sigh. His aunt chuckled, leading him over to a bench and telling him to sit while she got them some sweet breads from the baker near them.

"So." she cleared her throat once she handed him one of the pieces, sitting beside him before he could take a bite. "Who is this Scholar then?"

Chapter 13

He hadn't meant to stay so long. Perhaps a part of him hoped the longer he stayed, the more likely it would be that another nomad would come through. Seeing Piitridae had been a blessing and a curse in that way. A brief brush of a true return he was still unsure if he would ever see.

The generosity of the family meant he had more things given to him than he had planned for, and almost more than his packs had room for. A new warm cloak, leathers and shirts repaired and the ones that could not be salvaged to be left here for scrap and rags. Here, the price was in help bringing in the last of the harvest, a few days in the smoke houses preserving meat. He was glad for it, as he'd need all the coin he could manage to get back down to the trade routes, and to Port Morgranto to join a late caravan. Moving at his normal pace, he would catch nearly the last one if his memory served him right.

The weeks had been kind, putting weight on weary bones, even for Fish. If not especially, judging by his whining when he saw the travel bag being pulled onto Alnyx's shoulders.

"Don't look at me like that. You know as well as I do it's better for us to get going before we don't have a choice but to stay."

The beast snorted, and seemed to shake its head. But Alnyx knew he would follow when he left the borrowed room behind and walk to the center room of the family home.

"Mother said you'd be heading out on your way today." The cousin that had swooped in to save him from Saseshan's glares the day he returned was there, their bow and quiver by the door. Like they had been waiting for him to leave themselves. "Strict orders from her to make sure you see the Priestesses to get a blessing on your way out."

"Don't suppose I can get you to lie?"

"Absolutely not. Too much bad energy in that." they at least sounded a little apologetic about it.

They picked up their bow and quiver by the door, strapping everything into the correct spots as they made their way down the ramp. They didn't speak, a comfortable silence between the two of them as they made their way around children chasing one another and Watchers trying to keep them from too much trouble.

It wasn't a long walk to the edge of the settlement proper, though it was out of the way from the path Alnyx would have liked to have taken from The Grove to the trade-road. It made sense, though, that the Leyweavers and Priestesses kept themselves tucked further into the woods instead of out. His cousin paused at the gate that was a visual divide into the hallowed circle of trees, clearly not going further than that.

The two clasped forearms, whispering fond farewells as If anything in full voice would be an offense. Alnyx watched her go, tempted almost go to after. But, he was Expected. And they would know if he walked away this close.

So, he pushed the waist-high gate of birch branches open and stepped inside, fish trialing behind him on the left side. The closing of the gate behind them seemed to break a seal of some kind, the soft sound of water filling his ears from the fountain and statue in the center of the clearing. Carved of white stone, in the shape of the Lady of The Wood and Skyclad

Consort. A bowl held between them served as the fount, pouring down into a larger basin at their feet.

There knelt a figure that seemed too pale to be one of his kin. But the Leyweavers and Priestesses worked in the light of the moon. More like the cousins that ran off to their high towers in the East. The tattoos, visible under the intentionally thin shift they wore was the only true indication they belonged in the wood instead.

"Wanderer." her voice was only just louder than the bubbling of the fountain she didn't turn away from. "We have not seen you since the early days of your visitation."

"Apologies. I was caught up. There is always much work to do when I am here." Neither sentences were a lie. He shifted his weight from foot to foot when she didn't speak again. "I am going back out."

"You seek a blessing." Strong words, but he bit the inside of his cheek, to keep that thought to himself. "Come, sit. You will have one."

He hesitated only a moment. The thin, pale, woman, unbothered by cold even in her nearly-undressed state, unsettled him. Not her specifically; all her sisters did. And Fish didn't move a muscle. Traitor.

When she raised a thin hand to beckon him, he obeyed and moved beside her finally. She did not have to point on to the ground for him to kneel and finally face him properly. The unseeing eyes, milky white as the moon they often gazed at, pierced through him. He swallowed the flinch when her icy fingers touched his cheek.

"You have traveled far, Wanderer." she spoke with a voice that was and was not her own. "As we have said that you would. You have grown and learned."

He didn't respond. He knew she wasn't actually looking at him, wouldn't listen to him as her hands moved from his face to his shoulders. The probing push and pull of the weave was like being stabbed repeatedly with the needles that left their ink as they moved along the tattoos. They paused at the concentrated marks in the center of his throat.

"You have been busy."

"As I was told to be." he couldn't help himself this time. "As the Ancestors instructed. To be-"

"Wild and winded as the seed of a dandelion. To plant and grow in the lands Away from Us." She finished the words her sisters told him time and time again. "There is a change in you. A change that has gone Noticed."

There wasn't elaboration. Not right away. Alnyx had to fight the urge to rush her, to keep the impatience down. He closed his eyes when her grip tightened on his throat. As if she meant to choke the breath from him.

"An elk with no tines. A cacophony. The veil of the End and hem of her robes brush against you." This voice was a new one. Deeper. Primal. He couldn't recall hearing any such thing quite like it. "A silver storm rises, bringing dust and ash. You will chase the cyclone."

Wasn't there always some sort of wind in their words? In insult wrapped in the protection of prophecy. A cyclone, a storm, a gust that never pushed towards his Mother and Father. But to some new, some strange, place again and again.

She removed her hand from the column of this throat and leaned back. Blinking her sightless eyes, clearing her mind to return it to one more like her own. She turned her head back to the basin of water, cupping her hands into it, holding them up to Alnyx's face. In return, he leaned forward and parted his lips, drinking the too-cold water down. It stung as the Weave had.

"Find the storm. It comes for The Grove."

"Of course, Treespeaker." once he swallowed one last time, he stood again. "I will keep vigil, as wind and bone command."

"Do not falter." She spoke again with the soft voice that was and not hers. "The Skyclad Consort turns his gaze to you. He watches with great interest."

He couldn't stop the shudder, much as he tried. He looked to the statue where the water poured. For a moment, he could imagine the male in his furs with a poleaxe at his back but never dulled had turned its stone head to see him. Alnyx felt the need to keep his head low as he stepped back, arms across his chest in a proper showing of unarmed protestation before the figures.

As they walked from the hallowed ground, he kept a hand on Fish. Centering. Calm, warm against the chill in the air that had seemed to worsen. He was glad that the water was deafened on the other side of the gate.

* * *

Alnyx and Fish spent a few days at the outpost. Not for need of supplies, thanks to his generous family. There was an easy extermination job, some recaps that ran off from their master and were threatening the children of the Post. He took only half the coin, and insisted the supplies of fabric and preserved foods be returned to those who had offered them. Not this close to the cold.

The Taskers were always good for gossip when turning work over, which he was happier to trade in. The young man behind the desk said that "His" folk had come from the trees to talk to the mayor, and it had done good. Felt safer, more secure knowing that the humans weren't going to be hunted down in the night as long as they kept to where they were supposed to.

Unfortunately, there wasn't yet a change to the major cities requiring pairs of Taskers to take on jobs. Too much to hope for, he supposed. But, security for a trade route would be coin enough. And by the time the season shifted hopefully conditions would as well.

The third day he spent there was half of one, as snow had fallen in a measurable amount the night before. He hated to rush the travel; hated to needlessly tire himself, let alone Fish who would have been more than happy to stay in the ice.

"There you are! I was so worried that you were leaving ME for that terrible cold and stone. Two Northern contracts! I nearly had a heart-attack you jerk!"

"Marigold. Got something for me?"

www.ingramcontent.com/pod-product-compliance
Lightning Source LLC
Chambersburg PA
CBHW050422110726
47899CB00008B/2812